Rules of the (

SCORING CHANCE

RULES OF THE GAME BOOK ONE

EMMA THARP

Scoring Chance: A Second Chance Hockey Romance (Rules Of The Game Book One)

By Emma Tharp

Copyright © 2019 by Emma Tharp

For more about this author, please visit www.emmatharp.com

www.emmatharp.com

❀ Created with Vellum

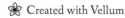

ONE

Cora

A LITTLE SIZZLE of nerves untangles in my belly before I knock on the door of the hotel room, wondering if it can be heard over the men's voices inside. This isn't just any hotel; it's The Preston, a five-star luxury hotel and one I don't visit often.

It's nothing like it used to be three years ago. Then, every time before a job I'd nearly throw up beforehand. Now it's not as difficult. Time and repetition tend to do that.

But it still sucks.

There are other places I'd rather be and other things I'd rather be doing, but none of them pay me as much money for such little effort.

And so it begins. I smooth down my barely there white dress and adjust my Marilyn Monroe wig. It's only an hour. I can do this.

Three loud raps on the door and the male voices get quiet as someone's footfalls get closer.

A tall guy with a large frame and spiky ginger hair answers the door. His pale green eyes scan my face and make their way to my ample cleavage and small waist, and of course he doesn't stop until he takes in my long lean legs. A slow smile builds across his lips and my cheeks heat up. "Marilyn, you made it. Right this way."

My knees go weak. The suite is full of tall, handsome men all in their mid-twenties to mid-thirties, some in suits, and others in dress slacks and shirts. There has to be at least twenty of them. I wonder what they do for a living; investment bankers, athletes, doctors, or lawyers. It's hard to say. The smell of cologne surrounds me, masculine and spicy. You'd think so many men together would create a strong smell, but somehow it doesn't. My mouth waters, an automatic response to the pheromones and testosterone thick around the room.

The ginger points to a man lounging in a leather chair. He's holding a glass with amber liquid and ice. He has thick dark hair and deep blue eyes, half-lidded with drink, no doubt the guest of honor. When his eyes land on me, he gets a devilish grin on his face. "Well, well. Who do we have here?"

I saunter over to him, pull my speaker out of my bag, sync it with my phone, hit play on my playlist, and start singing the first lines of "Diamonds Are a Girl's Best Friend."

Catcalls and clapping from the other guys erupt around us.

Kneeling in front of him, I run my finger up his leg and my hand lands on his thigh and I give it a squeeze before I turn around and bend over, giving him the perfect view of my white lace thong and bare ass. There's more cheering from around the room. Still facing away from him, I shake my booty, bouncing it in time with the song.

In my periphery, a handsome guy I hadn't noticed yet has his intense gaze locked on me. He seems familiar, but I can't place him. I wink at him and he smirks at me before I turn back in the direction of the guest of honor and straddle his lap, shimmying in his face I slide my dress up my thighs and he attempts to grab my hips. I give his hand a little whack and wave my finger in his face, giving him a warning that it's not okay to touch me.

When the song ends, the guy is in a daze worse than he was when I walked in. I play another song for him and dance, gyrate, and tease until I'm left in nothing but my bra and thong.

The guys love me. I've been told that I look like a real live Barbie. I guess that's a compliment, although it'd be nice to be appreciated for more than just my looks. Guess I'll have to pick a different career. Maybe someday. But for now I need this money.

I compartmentalize the irritation, annoyance, and sometimes anger I feel for the ogling men that think it's somehow okay to grab my ass or cop a feel. It wasn't easy at first, but now I consider myself an expert.

I find the next willing participant—the ginger who opened the door for me—I turn the music up and do a lap dance for him.

"Is this a bachelor party or someone's birthday?" I ask him as I grasp his tie and put my leg on his lap.

He grips the arms of the chair and inhales a sharp breath before he says, "Yeah, it's Slick's bachelor party."

Whipping my hair back, I jut my chest toward him and say, "How do you all know each other? Are you all college friends or co-workers?"

"I didn't mention it when I booked you, but we play for the Wolverines."

Holy shit. I should've guessed. Every single one of them has a tall, muscular, commanding presence. And here I am dancing for professional hockey players. I've always had a thing for jocks, even in high school, but I'm not dumb enough to fall for the likes of a professional athlete. Men who have women fawning over them and could have their pick anytime they'd like. No way. "That's great. I've never been to a professional hockey game."

The smile on his face is like a little boy's. It's as wide as they come and he's barely taken his eyes off my chest. "You should definitely come to a game. It's a good time."

"Maybe I will," I tell him before I shake my shoulders for him. Truth be told, I'd love to see a game, but I've never wanted to pay the money for a ticket.

Another song starts and it's my cue to dance for someone else. Ginger sticks a crisp one hundred dollar bill in the string of my thong. "I didn't catch your name," I say.

"I'm Teddy. You're very beautiful. Thank you for coming tonight," he says with a shy smile on his face, so different from the one he had a moment ago when I was on his lap.

"It was my pleasure to meet you, Teddy."

I do dance after dance for many of the team members; some are shy, some charming, and others you can tell deep down are assholes. Men get easier and easier to read as the years go by.

Turning, I go to the next chair over and I'm face-to-face with the gorgeous man with dark eyes from earlier. His suit is charcoal and it fits his lean, muscular form perfectly, highlighting his strong chest and toned legs. I'm drawn to him like a magnet. It's his masculinity, his familiarity. The air between us prickles and gets thicker, making it hard to breathe.

His gaze is intense. He's assessing me, taking me in, but not like the other men here. It's as if he can see through me. My pulse picks up and for a moment, I can't move. It's not like me. I'm never off my game at a gig.

I lick my lips and ask, "What's your name, handsome?"

"I'm Derek," he says, his eyes never leaving mine.

It's unnerving; the tone of his voice has an unmistakable rasp. I've heard it before. "Do we know each other, Derek?"

With a cock of his brow, he says, "You don't remember me?"

In that expression, the haze lifts. No way. I can't believe it. It's Derek Parker from high school. I tutored him in tenth grade math when we were both sophomores. I don't know how I didn't recognize him sooner. Maybe I blocked him out, like those sparkly toys I would always ask for at Christmas but never got. It's best to forget about them and move on.

I take a step back and he leans forward, elbows resting on top of his knees.

"You recognize me now, don't you? I can see it in your eyes."

He's changed since high school; he's still gorgeous, but now he's rugged with a sex appeal I'm sure no woman can resist. He's always been a jock, ultra-popular, and the entire female student body wanted him. The shy bookworm I was back then never got more than a sidelong glance from him until he needed to pass math to get into prep school. I always looked forward to our tutoring sessions. He had an easy charm and even though it was stupid, I let myself feel things for him, developing a stupid teenage crush. I was so naïve. "It's been a long time, Derek. How have you been?"

"You're right. How many years?"

He was a junior when he transferred out of our public high school. It's been ten years. I remember hearing that he got drafted to the NHL, but I didn't think he lived around here. "Ten years. You back in town visiting friends?" Without wanting to get too far out of character, I rest my heeled foot on his thigh, causing him to sit back all the way. If I dance for him and move on, I can keep him at arm's length. *It's just a gig, that's all this is.*

If I was trying to unnerve him, I haven't done a good job. An easy grin forms on his face as he scans my body on display for him. He glides a finger up the inside of my heel, never actually touching my skin, but it's as if he did because I'm momentarily off balance. I do my best to cover and thrust my chest toward him. He blinks and licks his lips. "Got traded. I live here now."

Pushing up off of him to get away from his sinfully sexy-smelling cologne, I spin around and say over my shoulder. "No touching," I warn. If his hands are on me for even a second, I don't know what I'll do. I can't trust myself after the reaction he caused from the simple act of touching my shoe. "Are you happy to be back in town?" Swinging my hips back, I bounce my ass to the beat of the music.

Derek leans to the side of the chair and he rests his arm on the armrest and props his cheek on his hand, giving him an air of nonchalance. Something deep inside me wants more of a reaction out of him. "Sure. Nashville is home."

Straddling his lap for the end of the song, I rake my fingers up the back of his hair. Our faces are mere inches from each other. His eyes burn through me and his stare is pure sex. I've had men look at me longingly daily, but not like this. This look sends a shiver up the back of my neck that nearly knocks me over. I have to blink.

The song comes to an end. I'm happy and sad it's over in equal measure. His nearness is turning me on and knocking me off-balance at the same time. It's a dangerous combination. One I have to steer clear of. "It was nice to see you, Derek. Have yourself a good night."

Climbing off his lap, I stand and check the clock. I'm booked for another ten minutes. One more dance with one more man and I am out of here. I excuse myself to no one in particular and go down a hallway I'm assuming leads to a ladies' room. The ceilings are high and the walls are stark white. It's a large suite with two bedrooms and at the end of the hall is the bathroom.

Once inside, I close the door behind me and lock it. Grasping the sides of the marble vanity I gaze at my reflection and can still feel the heat of Derek's stare covering me, surrounding me. It's how I always wanted him to look at me, but he never did. Now, he's an NHL player and I'm a stripper. Perfect. He must think I'm lower than low. This isn't how I saw my night going.

Regroup, Cora. It's just a gig. Get in. Get out.

I shake my head and send a silent prayer to whoever is listening that I won't see Derek again before I leave.

Unlocking, the door, I go to take a step out and Derek is right there, taking up all the space in the doorway and sucking all the air out of the room.

"Hi," he says. "Everything okay?"

"Sure. I'm fine." But the breathiness in my tone belies the words.

This man is pure, raw sexiness. From the tips of his dark hair all the way down to his expensive-looking designer leather shoes. Is my tongue hanging out? He's seriously throwing me off.

"Your cheeks are flushed." His finger sweeps over the skin of my cheek, and I know he's not exaggerating; my face is hot, like I've had it in an oven for the past hour.

"You're taller than I remember." His presence is all-consuming. I'm sure he could seem menacing if he came up behind you in an alley. He has to be at least six-five. I'd hate to be on the ice against him. I'm sure he can crush people.

The smirk that builds on his face is too damn sexy. "I grew up. And so did you." His eyes scan the length of my body, setting it afire once again.

"Not how you remember me?" I giggle but it sounds unnatural and fake.

"Nope. I think you always had on khakis and a sweatshirt that was two sizes too big for you. And didn't you wear glasses?"

Nodding, I cross my arms over my chest. All of the sudden I feel too exposed. "Yes. Looking back at old pictures, I'm not sure how my mom let me walk around with them. They were also two sizes too big. Maybe three."

Derek tips my chin up. I didn't even realize that my gaze had found its way to the floor. Leaning in, he says, "Why are you embarrassed? We aren't in high school anymore."

Heat creeps up my neck and I bite on my bottom lip. The

scent of his cologne is seductive: it's cedar and bergamot and clouding my mind. My emotions are all over the map. There's a part of me that wants to stand here with him all night and another that wants to run out of here like a scared rabbit.

This isn't how I was supposed to run into Derek Parker. It should've been on the street, me walking past him in my designer pencil skirt and blazer. Armani or Gucci, maybe. I'd be on my way from my office to go defend a client in court. He'd stop me and ask if I remember him. We'd hug and catch up for a minute. He'd be impressed by my accomplishments. Not like today. I'm sure all he has for me is pity. The smartest girl in high school takes her clothes off for money.

"Nope, you're right. We aren't. But I better get back out there. Your friends must be waiting for me." There's an edge to my tone that sneaks out. I didn't mean for it to sound so sharp and clipped. I turn on my heel but before I can take a step away, Derek grabs for my shoulder. His grip isn't rough, but firm and holds me in place.

"What the hell? Did I do something to piss you off?" His dark eyes narrow into slits and his eyebrows pinch together.

"No. No, I'm sorry if I'm being short with you." I conjure up what I can of a smile and take a deep breath. Derek isn't the reason for my shitty experience in school; in fact, he was one of the few people I looked forward to seeing when I was there. "I don't have great memories of high school and since I'm working, it's probably best if we don't talk about it now. And I'm sure you wouldn't understand, but I need this job. Please excuse me."

He drops his hand from my shoulder. Walking away from him, I feel his stare heat up my body from the inside. My stilettos click across the marble and I add more sway to my curved hips, giving Derek something to remember me by.

TWO

Cora

"YES, Mom. The restaurant was crazy. That's why I couldn't come home early." My throat always gets dry and scratchy like I've swallowed sandpaper when I lie to my sweet mother.

"It's good to have you home, sweetheart," she says. Her blue nightgown blends in so well with the couch that she almost looks like she's becoming a part of it.

Leaning down, I press a kiss to her soft cheek. "Sit up," I tell her. She does with some effort and I fluff the pillows behind her. "You didn't look comfortable. Is this better? Do you need anything?"

"I'm fine. Sit down and tell me about your day." She smooths her light gold hair away from her face. She could use a trim. I make a mental note to call her hair stylist and see if she can stop by. One more thing to add to the list.

Grasping the pillow next to me, I set it on my lap. "It was a zoo in there. I made great tips," I lie, but I can't tell her that I was stripping at a bachelor party. She'd die right here in front of me. The only job she thinks I have is at an Italian restaurant. If she knew about the real restaurant I work at, where I wear barely any clothes and dance on the bar for tips, she'd kill me. That is, if she still had enough strength to.

"What about men? Did any handsome businessmen come in and sit in your section? Maybe give you their numbers?" Her lips quirk up in a half smile.

I can't help but roll my eyes. I love my mother dearly, but the intensity with which she feels the need to marry me off always grates my nerves. "Nope. Nobody today," I say this as sweetly as possible, but it's difficult for me.

"Oh, I'm sorry. I didn't mean to upset you," she says. Her thigh jolts in a jerking movement and she nearly jumps off the couch. "Oh, damn." Tears form at the corner of her eyes.

Immediately I rub her leg, digging my thumbs into the weakened muscles that are taut in spasm and she slowly begins to calm. "Have you taken your evening pills?"

"Good Lord, no, I didn't. When I was watching TV earlier, I must've fallen asleep before I had the chance." The lines around her eyes turn down.

Damn MS.

It keeps getting worse.

"It's okay. Let me get you some fresh water." Standing, I grab her dinner plate off the coffee table and take it with me to the kitchen. It's important she doesn't see how upset I am. This disease is taking a damaging toll on my once active and vibrant mother and it guts me a little more each day that she has to suffer.

There's still half of the chicken breast and sweet potato on her plate I left for her for dinner. She needs to eat more. I take a few steadying breaths before filling her glass.

"Here you go." I hand her the pills from her evening pack along with the water.

She takes them from me and swallows them one by one.

"You'd tell me if things are getting worse, wouldn't you, Mom?"

Shaking her head, she says, "Everything is fine. Don't worry about me. You're doing a great job taking care of me. Your father would be so proud."

A metallic taste coats my mouth when I bite my tongue. She's so disillusioned about my father. Still. It's been five years since the hard-ass bastard died and she's still in denial about the relationship we shared. But I don't want to fight with my mother. Instead, I smirk at her and say, "Thanks. But please tell me if your symptoms get worse. We see the doctor next week and if we need to adjust your dosages or get a nurse to come in while I'm gone, we'll do it."

"How will we pay for that? No nurses and no nursing homes. The insurance doesn't pay for that. I'm fine." She crosses her thin arms across her chest.

A sick feeling churns around my stomach thinking about how much money we don't have. It's sad how little her insurance does pay. Most of her meds we pay for out of pocket, as well as her extra rehab and physical therapy visits, not to mention the modifications we've done to the house so she can still get around. I cringe to think where she'd be if I didn't have the jobs I do. How else would I pay for everything?

"Can I get you a snack or anything? You didn't eat much dinner."

Her hand comes to mine and she gives it a little pat. "I'd like to go to bed. I'm exhausted."

"Of course." I get up and pull her walker toward her and lean down. She puts her arms around my neck and I give her a boost. She can do this herself, but it's late and when her body is fatigued, it's best I help her.

We move in the direction of her room, and I'm close behind

her if she needs me. We go through her nightly routine. She brushes her teeth and I brush her hair. I tuck her in and kiss her forehead, the same as she did for me when I was a kid.

"Goodnight," I tell her as I turn off her lights.

"I love you, Cora."

"Love you, too."

"THAT SHIRT IS SEXY; I wish we were the same size. I'd borrow it," my best friend and co-worker, Brianne, says.

"Just wear three push-up bras instead of two and it'll work for you," I say.

Brianne swats my arm and groans. "Quit rubbing in that your boobs are huge and mine look like a twelve-year-old boy's chest."

"Ouch." She had some oomph behind that hit, even though she meant it to be playful. I rub the skin of my shoulder and she tilts her head back in laughter. "I wasn't rubbing in that my boobs are nicer. Bigger doesn't mean better."

"Ha! Tell that to the guys at Lolita's when I'm delivering them drinks. Even with the push-up bras, they'd all still say yours are superior."

I finish the last swallow of my cosmo and set the glass in front of me. It feels good to have the night off and have drinks with my girlfriend. It's good for my soul to laugh and be silly and not stress about work or my mother for an evening. It doesn't come without a healthy dose of guilt, but my mother has been hounding me to get out of the house and Brianne hasn't let up either about going out with her. I caved to both of them, and I'm so glad I did.

"Your body is beautiful and I don't care what anyone says. Steve never would've hired you if it wasn't," I tell her and mean it. She's tall, thin, with legs for miles. Sure, her bra size is a few smaller than mine, but she's still smoking hot.

"Jeez. Thanks. Now, enough about Lolita's. We're off tonight, so let's not talk about it. What else has been going on?" She crosses her smooth legs in front of her and flags down the bartender and signals for two more drinks. He nods and she flashes him her million dollar smile.

"A few nights ago, I had a gig at The Preston. A bachelor party."

Brianne's eyebrows couldn't get any closer to her hairline. "Holy shit. Must've been rich guys."

"Yeah. You could say that. It was the Nashville Wolverines hockey team."

At this exact moment, the bartender sets down our two martini glasses. Brianne's hand flies up and knocks them both over, sending pink liquid across the bar top.

"Are you kidding me? You lucky bitch. You danced for an NHL team?" she yells, completely oblivious to the fact that she just made a huge mess.

The bartender gives Brianne a dirty look and mops the mess up with a towel. I throw him an apologetic glance. "It wasn't as exciting as it sounds. It unnerved me and I didn't like it. Now tell the bartender you're sorry for spilling our drinks."

For the first time, she glances over her shoulder and sees the bar rag saturated in pink liquid. "Oh, no. I'm so sorry." She shrugs at the bartender and points her eyes back at me as if they were spotlights and she's interrogating me. "Spill. What had you so anxious?"

"It wasn't so much the team, but one of the players. Derek Parker. We went to high school together. I tutored him in math."

Bouncing up out of her chair, Brianne hurls her arms up to grab me by the shoulders at the same moment the bartender almost sets our drinks down again. Just in time he pulls them off the bar. "Hey, if you spill these, I'm going to have to charge you double." All the customer service niceties are gone.

"Oh, I'm really sorry," Brianne says in her sweetest voice, batting her eyelashes at him.

"It's okay. Be careful." He makes a show of setting the glasses down as gently as possible. Rolling his eyes, he walks away.

"We're going to have to leave him a good tip," Brianne says. "But enough about the drinks. Tell me what you know about the new superstar left wing for the Wolverines, Derek Parker."

I take several swallows of the smooth liquid before answering. "First of all, how do you know that? I didn't know that you were a hockey fan. And second, there isn't much to tell, other than the fact that I tutored him. He needed to get good grades to get into prep school. I helped him sophomore year and he got in and moved away our junior year. I never saw him again until last night." My insides heat up and not from the alcohol.

"Well, my ex-asshole loved to watch hockey and he was a Wolverines fan. Even though we aren't together anymore, I still love the game. But you need to explain why your cheeks are pink. Did you guys ever date?" she asks.

I touch my cheeks. Yup, they're warm. "No way. He was a player and I was a bookworm. We had nothing in common."

"Then what has you so flustered?" She runs her finger along the rim of her glass, but her eyes haven't left mine.

"Maybe it was the way he was watching me. I didn't recognize him at first and when I did a lap dance for him is when I finally made the connection." I turn my gaze from hers and look off in the distance, remembering how my body felt supercharged by electricity dancing for Derek.

"Hello." She snaps her fingers at me. "Where did you go? This guy got under your skin, didn't he?"

I shake my head, clearing myself out of the hot NHL player fog. "Sorry. I don't want to admit it, but I think he did. And he's the last thing I need to be thinking about," I say in a huff.

"Girl, what would be so wrong with thinking about a hot, available guy?"

"How do you know he's available?" I get that she watches hockey, but how does she know Derek's relationship status?

Brianne pushes her wavy brown locks over her shoulder and gives me her signature eye wink. "Yes, recently divorced. He's been playing more aggressively since the split. The commentators have been loving the story."

My nerve endings stand in readiness and start giving each other high-fives. I shiver and sit up taller. Why the hell should I be happy to hear that Derek got a divorce? Divorce is devastating and terrible. I remember firsthand how wrecked Brianne was when she was going through it. Yet here I am feeling like a kid on Christmas morning. "Wow. I didn't realize that hockey sportscasters were like that."

"They sure are. And you have a gleam in your eyes. Why don't you reach out to him? Get coffee or something? Wouldn't you like to catch up with him?"

"And say what? Yeah, my life went to shit? I dropped out of college and now I use my body to earn money?" My tone comes out whiny and pathetic and I'd like to slap myself for it.

"Seriously, you're kidding, right? You're so much more than that. Any man would be lucky to have a woman like you, who steps up to the plate when someone in her family needs help. I know it sucks that you didn't get a chance to finish college, but it'll always be there and you can finish someday." She lays a cool hand on mine, her long fingers covering it before she squeezes.

"You're right. I'm sorry. I hate when I get this way. Feeling sorry for myself gets me absolutely nowhere. But I won't be reaching out to Derek. I know how he was in high school. A total player who could have anyone he wanted. I'm sure not much has changed." I pick up my drink and let the alcohol warm my throat and dull some of the truth's sting. As attracted to Derek as I am, falling for him would get me nowhere and only serve as a distraction that I don't have time for.

Brianne raises her arm and tries to get the attention of the bartender, who walks right by us. "What a jerk. You spill your drink and then you get ignored. You almost ready to head out and go somewhere else?"

"Sure."

"Good, but before you we go, can I remind you that we aren't our pasts, okay? Even if it isn't Derek. Anyone and everyone out there has made mistakes; you shouldn't hold it against them. And I haven't seen you react this way in forever about a guy. He might be worth a phone call."

"Thank you for the reminder, but even if I wanted to call him, I don't have his number. But I do have tickets to see them play. Teddy gave me two tickets before I left the bachelor party. You want to go with me?"

She lets out squeal and exclaims without hesitation, "Umm, is that even a question?"

THREE

Derek

THE SQUAWKING, shrill sound coming from Coach's whistle signals it's time to get off the ice.

I'm not ready yet.

Wes must see it in my expression as I whack my stick on the ice, signaling to him to pass me the puck. Even though the play is over and so is practice, Teddy is still standing in the net. Wes sends the puck gliding over the ice right to my stick. Winding back, I channel all my aggression and energy into the shot and send it straight to the back of the net. Wes cheers and Teddy puts his gloved hand over his heart and sinks to his knees. "Practice is over, man. Let's get the hell out of here!" Teddy shouts.

"Give me the puck. One more shot," I tell him.

"Zamboni is waiting. Time to go, boys," Coach Stevens calls from somewhere behind me.

Fuck. I'd like at least another hour on the ice. It's the only time I'm not restless. No thoughts about Carrie. No what-ifs or could-have-beens.

I'm impatient. None of the guys are passing me a puck. "One more!" I shout to no one in particular.

"Fuck it, man. Let's get out of here," Slick calls from the bench. "Rose is having a girls' night. Let's do something."

"Just because your fiancée is busy doesn't mean that we have to do something. Now give me the puck. One more, then I'll leave." There'll never be enough ice time. I give it one hundred and ten percent every time I'm out here. No way am I going to take this for granted. I've seen it happen to too many guys. Some younger, better player is always waiting in the wings to take your place. I've been in the league for five years. I'm grateful for every practice and every game.

Slick must see something in my eyes because he throws a puck in my direction, and like clockwork, Teddy stands in the ready position. Gliding to my right and cutting left, I wind up and fake Teddy out. He goes down onto his knees in a perfect butterfly and I chip one up over his head, and it goes bar down behind him.

"Damn you, Rick! Why'd you have to give him another damn puck?" Teddy calls out as he skates off toward the bench. "I'm done for tonight."

Slick, Wes, and I, the only guys left on the ice, laugh at Teddy as we head toward the locker room.

"Let's go out. I need to get a drink and find myself a nice young lady," Teddy says as he pulls his goalie mask off his head, leaving his red hair standing straight up in a short wet Mohawk.

Wes plops himself on a bench and unties his skates. "Yeah, I'm game. Lydia is out of town at a gig. You going, Derek?" His dark eyes shoot me a "don't say no" look.

"I'm tired. Think I'll just go home," I say, without looking at any of the guys.

Slick throws a wadded-up ball of tape at me that hits the side of my head. "What the hell, man? You haven't gone out with us in forever."

He's right. I haven't because I'm over the going out scene. When Carrie and I got married, I settled into that life. If I was in town, we would stay home, just watch a movie, or cook dinner together. I loved it and was relieved that I wouldn't have to hang out in the over-crowded bars with women who barely know me, throwing themselves at me just because I play professional hockey. "I'm good. You guys go ahead."

"Don't you want to meet a nice lady, too?" Teddy asks, his pale green eyes and wicked grin urging me on.

The ink is barely dry on the divorce papers. I'm hardly ready to move on, yet it seems like the guys are ready for me to get right back on the horse. Funny how that is. Slick is getting married soon, Teddy is single, and Wes is dating Lydia Crow, a country music singer. Not one of them is qualified to give me advice or has any idea what I'm going through. "Nope, I'm in no damn hurry to find a random hook-up."

"Dude, don't you think that would ease some of the tension?" Slick asks as he takes off the last of his pads and wraps a towel around his waist.

"I think what Rick is trying to say is that we can tell you've been stressed out lately, on and off the ice, and we'd like to help you out. Even if it's just a couple of beers tonight to let loose." Wes swallows and runs his hand through his wavy brown unruly hair.

I exhale through my nose and focus on my feet. My friends are trying to help me out, and I appreciate that. The truth is that I have been stressed lately and tense as fuck. I never wanted to get a divorce, yet here I am still trying to pick up the pieces of the life I thought Carrie and I were living. It all blew up in my face before I'd even had a chance to try and fix it. "Why not? Let's go out for a few."

"Yes," Teddy says, hanging his giant leg pads up on the hook as he starts walking, bare-assed to the showers. "Let's go party."

THE CLUB IS a sea of bodies from one end to the other.

It's noisy and the reek of someone's cheap perfume hits my nose and turns my stomach. I move to the other side of Wes for some more breathable air.

I'm going to need a drink and fast.

Raising my hand up, I get the attention of the bartender and she stops in front of me, giving me a flirty smile. "Hey, handsome. What can I get you?"

"A round of tequila shots." I point toward the four of us.

She gives me a wink and walks away to get the bottle of Patron. She's cute in a pixie kind of way, but she's not my type. What exactly is my type? At this point, I'm not too sure. Maybe someone who brings out the best in me and can hang in there and work through problems instead of running when shit gets tough.

The bartender pours our shots and sets them in front of us. I hand her my credit card and tell her to start a tab.

We clink our glasses together and Teddy says, "Cheers to me getting laid tonight."

"We'll see, buddy." Slick slaps Teddy on the back before he tips his shot back.

Teddy's eyes turn down and he looks like Rick just ran over his puppy. "What the hell is that supposed to mean?"

We all laugh and I take my shot, welcoming the heat and sting.

"I'm just ripping on you, buddy. Let's find you a pretty lady."

Slick throws his arm around Teddy's shoulders and they turn out toward the dance floor.

"Well, hello, hottie," a tall blonde woman says, walking in my direction. Her fake tan shows up before she does. Her long hair is tied back in a ponytail and she's wearing a royal blue form-fitting dress. A large diamond pendant sits in her cleavage. Or is it a cubic zirconia? Fuck if I know. Her eyes are half-lidded and her manicured nail draws circles on my chest.

Taking a step back, I remove her hand and say, "Hi." My tone is tight and oozing impatience.

She eases closer, clearly ignoring my body cues, and takes my left hand in hers. "No ring. You looking for company?" Her breath smells of red wine, matching the blue tint on her teeth when she smiles.

Deep breath. Sometimes I think the universe is fucking with me. One easy night, a few drinks with my buddies. Seems it was too much to ask. My patience is low and my throat itches with wanting to tell this woman to leave me the fuck alone, but part of my job requires me to remain civil. To keep a professional persona when I'm off the ice. It's part of my contract. A few too many public disagreements when I was back in Toronto didn't go over well. Now I need to be a good boy and keep my nose clean. I'm going to do everything in my power to keep my job. The NHL is all I have left and nobody is going to take it away from me.

"I'm good, but Teddy here needs some companionship." I give her my million dollar grin and point her in Ted's direction.

Ted's eyes widen when the tan, blonde chick sidles up next to him.

I can't hear what she says to him, but he starts shaking his head and shoos her away. She looks back in our direction, a pout plastered on her face, and I can't help but laugh.

"What, dude? You too good for her?" I ask.

Teddy nudges me with his broad shoulder and says, "I need to get laid, but I have standards. She did not meet them. How old was she? Fifty?"

Wes snorts before chiming in, "She looked like your type to me. No dick, at least I don't think so."

Wadding up a cocktail napkin, Teddy chucks it at Wes's head. "I already told you that chick was hot. How could I have known she was a guy?"

I laugh and shake my head, remembering the time Teddy took home a transvestite. Poor bastard hasn't had the best luck with women. Come to think of it, neither have I.

Flagging down the bartender, I order a whiskey and relish the smooth oaky flavor of my first sip.

"I'll tell you who I'd like to get to know: the stripper from the bachelor party. I think her name was Cora. She works at Lolita's. We should stop in there next," Teddy says.

"How do you know where she works?" I ask, an exaggerated edge skidding off my tongue. I narrow my eyes at him. The thought of Teddy trying to hit on Cora rubs me the wrong way.

Teddy's head whips in my direction and he scans my face. "Woah. What the hell did I say?"

Sipping my whiskey, I take a second to collect myself. "I know her. From high school. You should keep your hands off her."

"Did you guys date or something?" Teddy's head is on a swivel between Wes and me.

Shrugging, Wes says, "I didn't know you knew the stripper."

Completely caught off guard hearing Cora's name, I overreacted and now their gazes are glued to me like I've got clues to find a hidden treasure. "She was my tutor in high school math. That's it. We didn't date."

"Why the hell not?" Slick chimes in. "She's hot as fuck."

For no apparent reason it irks me that the guys are talking

about Cora, calling her hot and a stripper. She's both of those things, but some twisted side of me feels protective of her. She's a good person who helped me out in school. That's it. She was my friend. Seeing her again, half naked, lit up parts of me that I'm still trying to figure out. "Can we not do this? She was a friend of mine and calling her a stripper is annoying me."

"But...she is, man," Teddy quips.

My insides seethe and I'm overcome with the desire to grab Teddy's shirt, throw him up against the bar, and kick the shit out of him. I won't do it, but, man, do I want to. He shoots his hands up over his head and backs away. "I mean no offense. She seems nice. In fact, why don't we get out of here and head over there now?"

She could be working. I could possibly see her tonight. Heat spreads up my limbs. But does she want to see me again? It certainly didn't seem like she wanted anything to do with me at the bachelor party. I've been thinking about that night and there are no logical answers for why she was so standoffish. Like she didn't know me, and after I introduced myself, she acted like I was something gross stuck on the bottom of her shoe. I should be pissed at her reaction, but it's quite the opposite. I'm intrigued.

Pounding the rest of my drink, I slam my glass on the bar and say, "Let's go."

I'm unreasonably excited when we walk into Lolita's. It's been forever since I've been here. Before I left for Toronto. It's the same as it was before. Huge oak bar, stage, dance floor, but tonight none of it matters. My eyes scan the place for her. Fuck. She isn't here. I immediately want to leave. But my friends would know something was up if I told them it's time to leave before we've even had a drink.

Suddenly I'm too tired to deal with it all. The crowds of people, the unwanted attention from random women. All of it.

We find a spot at the bar and Wes orders us a pitcher. A well-endowed bartender sets four glasses in front of us and takes Wes's credit card with a wink. Pouring myself a pint, I suck down half of it and hunch over the bar.

"She's one of the hottest chicks I've ever seen." Slick whacks me on the back, pulling me out of my bad mood. I turn toward where he's looking and there she is, like a tall glass of water in the desert. "What's her name again?"

I don't tell him. Instead, I make my way toward her. She doesn't notice me. She's talking to a group of biker guys at a table. It's only a second before she turns and stops short, slamming into me.

Cora's hands come up to her mouth. "Derek." Her tone is breathless, like she just ran a marathon. She never expected to see me here.

FOUR

Derek

"HI, it's good to see you again," I say.

It takes her a few seconds to compose herself, but the slight grin on her face falls away and the mask she wore the other night is firmly back in place. "Can I help you?"

"Yes, could my friends and I get a table please?" I say, allowing my eyes to take her in. Just as gorgeous as I remember her. Long legs in her jean shorts, a red plaid shirt tied up under her breasts, cleavage up high. Blood rushes to my groin the same way it did when she danced for me at the bachelor party.

She looks around. I'm not sure if she's looking at tables or if she's trying to see if I actually did come with friends. "Sure. Let me set something up."

When she walks away, I grab her shoulder, turn her toward me, and say, "In your section."

There's surprise in her features, her wide eyes, and arched brows. "Oh, okay. Give me a minute. I'll come get you."

As promised, she saunters over to the group of us and wags her finger in our direction, signaling us to follow her. We grab our beers and make our way to a table in the corner. She hands us menus. "Do you boys need any drinks?"

"Nice to see you again, Cora." Teddy goes up to her and plants a kiss on her cheek as if they were long-lost friends and didn't just meet a week ago at a bachelor party.

Cora's face brightens into a sexy smile. For Teddy. She didn't give me that smile. "Good to see you, too, Teddy," she says.

"We'll take another pitcher and fifty hot wings. And a pizza, too," Teddy says.

Writing our order down on her pad, she says, "Got it. I'll get this right in for you." She winks at him and walks away.

A smile and a wink. What the hell? There's no way I can be jealous of Teddy, but I wish she'd look at me that way instead of him.

The worst part is that I have zero clue what I might've done or said to her to deserve the cold shoulder. Have I offended her somehow? It's possible. I wasn't known for my manners back in high school, but surely she isn't holding that against me.

My memories of her in school are good ones. I liked her. But she must've thought I was an idiot. Without her help, I never would've made it through math.

"You okay, man? You seem off tonight." Wes sits next to me, beer in hand and a concerned expression on his face. Of all of my teammates, Wes is the most like a brother to me. I trust him. From day one, we got each other. He plays right wing and I'm left. We're on the same line and play flawlessly together. It's been this way since college. And when I got traded to Nashville I was thrilled to be playing with Wes again.

"Yeah, I'm okay. But for some reason, Cora's getting under my skin. She was my tutor in school, and now she acts like I've got a contagious disease. It doesn't make sense."

"Did you guys have sex?" he asks.

Finishing the last of my beer, I set it on the table in front of me. "No. We didn't even date. The woman you see now isn't the girl she was back then."

"What do you mean?" Wes pours me a fresh glass of beer from the pitcher and tops his off.

"She was reserved and shy, but don't get me wrong, she's always had a way about her that was endearing and sexy. Her walk, her no-nonsense attitude, except back then she covered her body with baggy clothes. Almost as if she didn't want anyone to notice how perfect it was," I say, shaking my head at the memory of some of the things she'd wear.

Leaning his elbows on the table, he says, "What's her story?"

"That's the thing. I don't know. Since I was a junior when I left to go to prep school, I didn't keep in touch with her after I left. She wasn't an open book, either," I tell him.

"From a quiet book nerd to a sexy stripper. Doesn't make sense. If she was smart enough to tutor you, why the hell didn't she end up in college with a career?" He scratches the side of his head, fingers mussing his wavy brown hair.

Blowing out a long breath, I say, "Hell if I know."

Cora sets a basket of wings and a new pitcher on the table. Slick and Teddy are now playing darts and Wes whacks me on the back and says, "Be right back."

"Wow, didn't mean to make everyone leave. People usually don't take off when I bring the food and drinks." Cora has a mock offended look on her face.

"They didn't leave because of you. They're just doing their own thing for a few." Moving in to get closer to her, I say, "I wanted to ask you the last time I saw you, how have you been?"

Her eyes widen at my proximity. "I'm great. How about you?"

I'm close enough now to smell her perfume. I'd like to touch her skin; it looks smooth and soft. "Not bad. It was nice to see you at the bachelor party."

She's biting her perfectly full bottom lip and staring at my chest. "Yes, it was."

For some reason a buzz of nerves flares up and I grip my beer to stop my hand from shaking. "What do you say we get together sometime? To catch up."

"No. I'm really busy. I have to go check on your pizza. Be right back." She spins on her heel and takes off like I just told her someone has a bomb at the table.

Fuck me. What is up with this woman? When I come on to a woman, they accept my advances. They don't run away. Well, with the exception of Carrie, soul-sucking woman that she is. Why do the women I want the most want nothing to do with me?

A half-dressed woman with long curly red hair makes her way toward me. "Hey, need anything? I'm helping out with Cora's tables."

"You work here, with Cora?" I ask.

She gets closer and makes no move to disguise her approval of me. Her pupils dilate and her tongue glides over her top lip. "Sure do. My name's Lonnie." She places her hand in mine and we shake.

Lowering my voice, I lean in and give her the smile all my female fans love. "Good to meet you, Lonnie. Mind if I ask you a question?"

Her fingertip grazes my forearm. "Sure."

"Is Cora dating anyone?"

A flash of disappointment crosses her face, but just as quickly, she recovers and says, "Not that I know of. She's a sweet girl, but very private. Why, you interested?"

"We knew each other. A long time ago. It's as if she's a different person now." Who knows why I'm spilling my guts to

Cora's co-worker. I hope Lonnie will see my vulnerability and share what she knows.

Her head swivels around behind her and scans the area to see who's around. "I just started working here a few months ago, but I really like Cora. She's sweet when she opens up to you, but she has a tough exterior. Her mother is sick. She takes care of her. Works her ass off here and some stuff on the side. Please don't mention that I told you anything, okay?" Her words spill out fast and full of regret, like she wishes she could take them all back and stuff them down her bra like a tip some dude just gave her.

"Don't worry. I won't tell her a thing about our little chat. I appreciate it." I tug a pen from her apron and slip it behind my ear before I walk away.

The bathrooms are covered in signs of bands coming to play, apartments for rent, and one paper captures my attention. It's a charity auction. You can win a date with one of the waitresses from Lolita's. I pull it off the wall, fold it, and tuck it in the pocket of my jeans.

Back at the table, Wes is there and Cora is setting a pizza in front of him.

Her barely-there jean shorts ride high on her legs, highlighting her round ass. All I want to do is touch her and feel the smooth skin of her shoulders under my fingers. I can see it now, the tension there in her muscles. She's taking care of her mother. What happened to her? Is she ill? The desire to take care of Cora, like she took care of me in high school, grabs hold of me.

I take the paper out of my pocket and rip the corner off. Using the pen I took from Lonnie, I jot down my cell number.

Stalking up behind Cora like she's an innocent gazelle and I'm a cheetah going after my prey, I come up behind her and press my chest to her back and move her hair away from her ear. She startles, but I whisper, "Shhh. It's just me, Derek."

She sucks in a sharp breath when I slip my hand around the curve of her hip and tuck the paper with my number on it in the right front pocket of her shorts. She doesn't move.

The heat from her body against mine and the smell of her rose perfume has me fantasizing about what it'd be like to have her in my bed, naked under me, skin against skin. "I want you to call me. Anytime. Day or night. If you need anything or want to talk."

She twirls around, eyes scrutinizing me. "You want me to call you?" Her words come out throaty.

"Yes."

Her eyebrows shoot up and she nods slowly. "Okay."

The last thing I want to do is scare her away, and right now she looks like I am going to pounce. I lower my voice and do my best to soften it. "There's nothing to be afraid of, Cora. I'd like to catch up with you. I'm asking for a conversation."

"But, I'm really b—"

I stop her before she can finish the sentence. "I get it. Your life is crazy. That's why I said anytime. I meant it. Don't say no. Think about it."

It'd be great if she'd give me her number but I know that's not going to happen. She has her guard up. In fact, I'll be surprised if she calls me at all.

Cora stands up straighter, rolls her shoulders back, and gives me her generic, "I'm a waitress who's tired of small talk" smile. "Enjoy your pizza. Let me know if you need anything else."

Before Wes or I can say anything, she walks away.

A few more beers later and the guys and I are playing darts. My eyes are drawn to Cora wherever she is in the bar. She's caught me staring at her numerous times. She acts like she's ignoring me, but I know she isn't.

Some older guy with his gray hair in a bandana and a biker

jacket on is calling Cora over to his table. She's busy with another table, but when she's free she makes her way over to the old guy. They talk for a minute and as she walks away from him, he palms her ass and squeezes it and sends her off with a whack. She shakes her head and flinches in disgust. She doesn't turn around and say anything to the guy even though she clearly didn't want him to touch her.

Everything comes to a grinding halt. All I want to do is throw my fist into that asshole's face. I stalk toward him and tap him on his shoulder.

He looks up at me. I'm at least a foot taller. "Can I help you?"

"Yup. You need to keep your fucking hands off her," I sneer and point in Cora's direction near the bar.

"What the hell, dude? Is she your girl or something?" He stumbles back one step, but I close the distance.

Clenching my fists at my sides, I say, "It doesn't matter what she is to me. She doesn't want you touching her. Am I clear?" Spit flies out of my mouth with the last words and I've drawn the attention of a couple of his biker buddies.

"Do we have a problem here?" a man with a massive beer belly and the same leather jacket as his comrade asks.

I take a deep breath and puff out my chest. I could crush both of these has-beens with one punch each. If they'd leave Cora alone, it'd be worth it.

"Hey, hey, guys. Can I help you?" A hand comes up to my shoulder as Wes approaches the scene.

"These jackasses think it's okay to touch Cora when it really fucking isn't." The drink has loosened my lips and inhibitions. I'm seconds away from a bar fight, and Wes is the only reason I'm not already swinging.

"I think these guys wouldn't mind telling Cora they're sorry and keeping their hands to themselves, would you now?" Wes towers over the gray-haired guy as he slaps him on the back, forcing the guy forward a step. He looks like he might piss himself any minute.

Mister beer belly puts his palms up toward Wes and says, "We mean no harm to anyone. I'm sure Gary and I can finish up our drinks and head out for the night."

"What's going on, guys?" Cora asks, her tray full of a round of drinks.

"It looks like Gary and his friends won't be needing those drinks. They're just heading out. Isn't that right?" Wes takes one of the drinks off the tray and takes a sip.

"Yeah, we've gotta head out. Early morning tomorrow." Gary puts his arms over his head and yawns. "You boys enjoy our drinks. They're on us."

Wes takes the tray out of Cora's hand and walks it toward our table. I turn to walk away, too, before I do something I will regret, like push Gary to the ground and kick his head in.

"Wait." Cora grabs my arm. "Seriously, what was that all about?"

I consider lying to her, but why bother? "I had to say something to that asshole for smacking your ass. It was uncalled for."

She blinks at me, clearly baffled. "That's not your job. You don't have to do that."

I massage my temples and pinch my eyes shut. "I know it's not my responsibility. It's yours. Why didn't you tell him not to touch you? I saw it in your face. You didn't like it. He has no right."

"Derek." She pokes a finger in my chest. "This is my job. I need it. I can't have you coming in here and arguing with regulars. You could get me fired. "

"Why don't you get a new job?" I huff out.

She gives me a hard stare, eyes full of anger, disappointment, and humiliation. "You don't know anything about me. Don't walk in here and pretend like we're friends. We aren't. Now I have to get back to work. Could you please try and not get me fired tonight?" And with that, she gives me a scowl and clicks off in her stilettos.

FIVE

Cora

"A RELAXING EVENING is just what the doctor ordered." I tap my wine glass to Brianne's.

"Ok, well, dinner will be relaxing. The hockey game later won't be," Bri says.

It's been two weeks since Derek and his teammates came in to Lolita's and I haven't been able to stop thinking about him. An unhealthy amount of my free time has been devoted to thinking of Derek's body pressed against mine, his strong hand on my hip when he slid his number in the pocket of my shorts. My heart rate accelerates and a pulse pounds between my legs at the memory of it.

"What's the dumb grin on your face for?" Brianne raises her forkful of tonight's fish special—herb roasted filet of sole—to her mouth.

Oh, no. She caught me. I'm sure my cheeks are an unflattering shade of red. "Nothing. I mean, I'm excited for the game. That's all."

"You're excited to see Derek. Don't even try to deny it."

Shaking my head, I say nothing.

"You should be excited to see him," Brianne says. "I'm still impressed with him for standing up to the biker dudes. They really shouldn't have grabbed your ass. I don't let them touch me."

That's why she doesn't make as much money as I do. The screeching need to make more, do more, doesn't keep her up at night like it does me. "I know. I'm glad it ended when it did. Can you imagine if Derek laid one of them out? I could lose my job, or worse, he could get arrested and who knows what would happen with the team. I'm sure they don't look on getting into bar brawls too kindly."

Her eyes get round like saucers. "I never thought of that. But it ended up fine. Nobody got hurt and I think the assholes got the message."

"True." I run my finger along the edge of my wine glass.

"And can we talk for a second about the fact that he must have feelings for you? Not just anyone would do what he did."

"Let's not go jumping to conclusions. I'm sure he looks at me like I'm a little sister. Not to mention, he had too much to drink. He wouldn't act that way if he were sober." As I say it, even I don't believe it, but I can't allow myself the luxury of guessing what his motives are.

Throwing her head back, she laughs. "Okay. Is that why I saw him come up behind you and whisper in your ear?"

"You saw that?" I didn't realize anyone noticed. Especially her.

Brianne rips a piece of bread off the loaf and douses it in olive oil. "Sure did. It was shameless flirting."

"I don't have time for any of that. Nor do I need a guy in my life. They all suck anyway." My words come out in a rush. Pent-up emotions come bubbling to the surface.

Grabbing my hand, Bri gives me a sweet smile. "Just because you haven't had luck with men in the past doesn't mean they're all assholes looking to use you. You need to start dating again." She's being sincere, but her advice is too much for me right now.

"With what time? I'm working and taking care of Mom. She is what I need to focus on."

"I know. That's all you focus on. She loves you for it, but I also know that she wants more than anything for you to be happy," Bri says.

Wouldn't that be perfect? To have a prince on a white horse swoop in and rescue me. But that's never going to happen. This is all on me.

Sitting up straighter, I cut my steak, but before I can put a bite in my mouth, I set the silverware down.

"Stop it," Brianne says, and there's a note of empathy in her tone, but also the slight edge of impatience. "You can't do this."

"Do what?"

She makes a sweeping gesture around her face. "You get all up in your head and then you don't have a good time. I'm sorry I brought it all up. Let's quit talking about Derek and men and all of it."

"That's a great idea." I lift my glass and she lifts hers. We clink them together. Even though we aren't going to talk about him now, I'm sure it won't stop the banter as soon as we get to the game.

And as predicted, as soon as we get to the arena and find our seats, Bri is right back at it. "I love watching warm-ups. Don't they all look hot? There's Derek over there. Number ten." She points her finger at him.

Despite the cooler temps in the rink, my entire body heats up.

As if I didn't know immediately by watching his gorgeous body gliding across the ice, winding up to slam pucks into the net. I can tell even without looking at his jersey number, although I knew he was number ten before she told me. Information gleaned from my shameless Internet stalking. To me, it's obvious who Derek is, even in pads and a helmet. "Oh, really?" I say with an air of nonchalance.

She turns toward me and rolls her eyes. I can't put much past her.

"Can you believe how close our seats are?" Bri says before shoving a handful of popcorn into her mouth.

"They are impressive." Sitting this close to the glass and the team's bench sets a slew of butterflies free in my belly. Especially when the guys finish warm-ups and Derek makes his way to the bench. His eyes find mine, he winks at me and gives me a delicious heart-stopping smile. My insides melt, but a sliver of worry works its way into my mind. Worry that I'm letting Derek get to me.

Bri nudges me in the side. "I saw that."

All I can do is shake my head. Of course she saw it. And she's not going to let me forget that he winked at me either. "I need a drink." Getting out of my seat, I make my way to the beer vendors and head back in to the rink double-fisted.

This is intense. I've never seen a live NHL game before and I wasn't prepared for the buzz that comes with the noise and energy in the arena. Nashville fans cheer with enthusiasm when the team scores and shout and boo when one of the team members gets put in the penalty box.

An all-time high for me is when Derek comes around the back of the net and sneaks a puck under the goalie's pads with less than a minute left in the game. The crowd goes absolutely nuts because that goal puts us in the lead. The thrill of being here mixing with the alcohol sends my head in the clouds. It's almost as if my boyfriend just scored. I'm out of my seat, nearly jumping up and down. A group of guys sitting next to me give me high-fives in celebration.

Bri and I join the sea of people leaving the arena. "I don't know about you, but I can't wipe the smile off my face." Bri grabs my arm and we weave around a particularly slow couple.

"Agreed. The game was amazing," I say. It's been forever since I've been in this good of a mood or had this much of a buzz.

"Where do you want to go now?" she asks.

I'm too amped up to go home and go to bed, and I arranged for my neighbor to go check on Mom and help her to bed. I already received a text that said Mom is doing great and I should enjoy myself tonight. "Let's go out."

We get a taxi to take us downtown and on the way, Bri gets a text. "Holy shit. Teddy wants us to meet them—the entire team," she emphasizes the last part. "At the Rooftop Bar. It's reserved, but he said he'll leave our names at the front."

All at once my grin widens and a charge of excitement tingles to life inside me. I'm going to see Derek tonight. At the game all I could think about was how much I'd like to talk to him again, be in the same space as he is. Of course, I know we'll never be more than friends to each other, but it doesn't matter. Tonight I want to flirt with him; maybe he'll even touch me again, like he did when he put his number in my pocket. It could be the alcohol, but I let out an uncharacteristic yelp. "Sir, we need to go to the Rooftop Bar, please," I tell the driver.

"Now that's what I'm talking about," Bri says. "My girl is here and ready to party."

"Yes, I am. Just like you said. Let's have fun tonight."

The doorman is at least six-seven, maybe taller, and he has the stone-cold stare down to a science. He barely makes eye contact with us until Bri saunters up to him and flips her hair over her shoulder. "This is my friend Cora Locklyn, and I'm Brianne Jacobson. We should be on the list."

He doesn't even look at us, but he consults the clipboard in his hand, scans it, and unhooks the black rope divider as he lets us go by.

"Nice guy," I whisper to Bri as we walk down the hallway and up the stairs to the roof.

It's magnificent. The bar is in the shape of a U. There are tower propane heaters at all four corners of the space and the lantern lights cast a glow all around the bar.

The hockey players aren't here yet, but the patio is full of people. Good-looking people, I might add. Tall men, women in short skirts and tight dresses. There doesn't seem to be anyone let in this bar unless you meet a minimum attractiveness standard. Smoothing my hands down my hips, I'm self-conscious about my skinny jeans and red V-neck top. Maybe I should've gone home and changed.

We find a spot at the bar and scurry to take it before someone else does. I gesture to the bartender when she looks in our direction and she comes right over to us. "Two beers," I tell her.

She nods and walks away.

"This place is fantastic," Bri says, her mouth slightly agape as she scans the area, clearly as impressed as I am.

"I can't believe I've never been here before. Didn't even know it existed." I reach across the bar to take the beer I ordered. Digging through my purse, I hand her my credit card and she smiles and waves it away.

"This is a private party. Drinks are on the house."

Bri's brown eyes widen. "Can you believe this? First, we sit next to the glass at an NHL game, and then we get invited to a party at the Rooftop Bar where drinks are free. This night just keeps getting better and better."

I nod, give her a wink, and take a swallow. She's right. I have a good feeling about tonight. Now if only Derek would show up.

The beer goes down easy and I've just ordered another one when out of the corner of my eye, I catch a glimpse of Derek walking through the entrance. He's in a form-fitting suit, his dark hair perfectly styled as if he didn't just play an aggressive game of hockey. A gorgeous dark-haired woman stops him. Her fingers slide along the length of his bicep. He smiles at her, but it's not genuine. She leans in close to him and whispers something in his ear. My skin crawls. I don't like her touching him, getting so close to him. *Why am I being territorial?* He isn't my boyfriend.

Derek's eyes look up and find mine. He puts his finger up and nods at the woman he's speaking to before he walks away from her. He comes toward me, closing the distance between us. His broad shoulders are set back and his confident gait stalks toward me. I can't look away.

SIX

Cora

LEANING IN, Derek kisses my cheek and pulls back to give me a once-over. The hair on my nape stands to attention.

"It's good to see you, Cora. I'm glad you could make it." He's still close enough for me to smell his cedar and bergamot cologne. Absolutely mouth-watering.

"Thank you, or should I say Teddy, for inviting us. And also for the seats. The game was amazing."

His face lights up in a boyish grin at the compliment. "You're welcome. And it was a great game to see live. The crowd was into it since the score was so close."

"I was worried, but when you scored the last goal, I stood up and cheered I was so proud of you." Normally, I wouldn't open up and say things like this, but since I've had a few drinks, I seem to be loose-lipped. *Screw it, it's all about having fun tonight.*

"You must've been my good luck charm. You're going to have

to come to all my games." His expression is playful, but his tone has a serious note to it.

I tilt my head back and laugh. "Right."

Derek moves in closer and puts one of his hands on the bar as the other signals the bartender. She comes over and shamelessly bats her eyes at him. Can't blame her. He's incredibly good-looking, standing here in his expensive clothes with his tall muscled body underneath it. Everything about the man screams sex appeal. He must have a cult of women who idolize him, dropping their panties at his request.

He orders a club soda. "I don't drink very much. Sorry about the other night at Lolita's. I was out of line." His lips form a tight line and it's clear that he's still not happy about seeing Gary grab my ass.

"It doesn't make sense to me, but I accept your apology."

"Thank you," he tells me without going into more detail.

The bartender hands Derek his drink. He drops a one-hundred dollar bill on the bar and says, "What do you say we go play a game of pool?" He gives me flirty, playful smile that immediately lightens the mood.

"I'd love to." Pool is a game I am actually quite good at. Years of practice during down time at the bar might come in handy tonight.

Looking over my shoulder, Bri is in a conversation with Teddy. I whisper to her that I'll be back soon. She winks and gives me a wave.

With Derek's hand on my back, we walk toward the pool table. His touch is electric, even in such a simple gesture.

"You look good tonight." His dark eyes assess me.

Heat spreads up my neck. On a shaky exhalation, I say, "Thank you. You're looking handsome tonight, too." It's a gross understatement; he's rip your clothes off and lie down anywhere kind of captivating.

Strolling over to the rack of pool sticks, he gets one and comes back to stand next to me. "What do you say we make the game interesting with a bet?"

My mouth is suddenly too dry. "What do you have in mind?"

He chalks up the end of the stick and sets it down, leaning against the table. "If I win, you have to give me your number. Wait, that's too easy. If I win, I get a date with you."

"I don't date," I blurt out.

His eyes widen at my sudden outburst. "Why not?"

"I'm really busy with work and everything. I barely have time for myself. It's sad actually...." I'm rambling and I know it. His gaze won't let go of mine. I peer down at the floor.

"It's okay. Relax. How about if I win you give me your number?" he says.

"What if I win?"

Tapping his fingers against the pool table, he says, "I'll get you tickets to another home game. How does that sound?"

I want to throw my arms around him. But I don't. Instead I nod, a huge smile spreading across my face and say, "That sounds good." I turn and go to the edge of the table and rack the balls. "You want to break?"

He has an impressed expression on his face and hands me the stick. "You go ahead."

Taking it from him, I lean over the table, bat my lashes a few times, and set up my shot. Hitting the cue ball hard, the rest roll around the table and the two ball goes into the side pocket and the four into the right corner. Solids.

"Nice job," Derek says as he removes his suit jacket and rolls up his sleeves.

Quit staring, Cora.

Assessing the table, I look for the perfect opportunity to sink a ball and situate myself in front of Derek. It's a tricky shot, but I think I can do it. "Seven in the side pocket." I point out the route

I'm going to take with the end of my stick and lean down directly in front of him. He makes no move to shift out of the way. Perfect.

I stick my hips back as far as possible, giving him a front row view of my ass. Now I'm thanking my lucky stars that I did wear jeans. This pair highlights all of my assets.

Taking my time, I line up the shot. I am slightly distracted by the heat of his gaze behind me, but the shot goes right in.

"Woo. That was a nice shot." Derek lifts his beer and takes a swallow.

Adding more chalk to the end of my stick, I study the table.

Derek comes up behind me. His breath sweeps over my right shoulder, sending chills all the way down my back. Taking the stick out of my hand, he points it at the table. "What if you aim the cue here and send it this way to sink the five?"

It won't be easy, but I like a challenge. Taking the stick from him, I lean over and line it up. Derek leans over me, the hard lines of his body flush against mine, his huge hand wrapping around mine. I'm acutely aware of every inch of his body covering mine. A shot of pure adrenaline spikes through me and it's nearly impossible to stand still, but I do my best.

"See what I mean?" The tone of his voice is seductive in my ear. He moves the back of the stick with his back hand, still guiding mine with his front hand, mocking up the shot he thinks I should take.

"Yes," I say, my voice breathy.

He moves away from me and I instantly miss the contact.

Unable to focus and thrown off my game, I aim and miss the shot. Damn. I want to win.

Derek takes the stick out of my hand and says, "It was a tough shot. Nice try."

The disappointment I felt moments ago at missing is replaced quickly with admiration. Damn, hockey players have perfect asses.

His body is a portrait of male perfection and this up close and personal view is stirring up sexual desire that I haven't felt in a very long time. Crossing one leg over the other, I lean against a nearby table in an attempt to dull the ache building between my thighs.

Derek sinks four shots in a row and before he takes his fifth shot, he looks up at me, locking eyes with mine and shoots, making an absolutely impossible shot look like child's play.

His last shot is for the eight ball. It'll be simple for him. My heart rate picks up. I'm going to have to give him my number. What will that mean? It's too dangerous.

At the last second, he hesitates and nicks the corner of the cue ball, sending it in the wrong direction and away from the eight ball. There's no way he should've missed that shot.

"Damn," he says and hands me the stick.

I give him a questioning stare, but he just shrugs and lifts his beer to his lips.

The rest of my shots aren't too difficult. When I set up the last shot, I put all of my concentration into it. I do love to win. "Eight ball in the side pocket," I tell him and pull back on the stick, giving it just the right amount of momentum. The ball follows the path I set for it and sinks into the pocket. Standing up to my full height, I set the stick down on the table and spin around and do a little dance, shaking my ass.

Derek comes up to me and wraps his arms around me, squeezing me close. I bury my face in his chest and smell his clean scent. My entire body heats up and I look up into his face.

"Great win. You earned your next set of tickets," he says and leans in to kiss my cheek right next to my ear.

My legs go liquid and the urge to turn my face and line our lips up is almost unbearable.

Pushing back off of him, I say, "Thanks, even though I think you gave it to me."

His hands go up. "Nope. You won, fair and square. You'll have to give me your address so I can mail them to you."

Part of me is sad that he's going to mail them to me since I'd like nothing more than to see him again face-to-face, but this way is definitely best. "Of course. That'd be great."

The rest of the evening goes by in a blur. I meet Derek's teammates and it's much less awkward now that I have my clothes on. They are all kind to me and don't treat me with disrespect. It's a nice change from the way most men treat me once they know I'm a stripper. It wasn't that long ago that I stripped for them at Rick's bachelor party.

At last call, Bri and I decide to call a cab. "No way. My driver will take you wherever you want to go," Derek insists.

"Sounds like a plan to me," Bri says, her words slightly slurred. "I'm going to say goodbye to Teddy before we go."

"That'd be great, if you don't mind," I say.

"Not at all." Derek grabs me around the waist and kisses me in the same spot as he did earlier, on the cheek, right next to my ear. I almost lose my legs again and have to hold him extra tight for support. And too soon he pulls away and reaches for his cell phone. "Give me your information so I can get you your tickets."

I tell him my address and he types it in. "Perfect. My driver is downstairs waiting; he's in a black Tahoe, tinted windows. Thanks for coming tonight. It was nice spending time with you."

"Yeah, it was. Thank you for having us. I look forward to another game," I say.

"Of hockey or pool?"

"Both." I grin before I turn and walk away to find Bri.

SEVEN

Derek

"WHAT'D you think of my last save last night? I couldn't believe it was in my glove, the way I landed on my ass like that." Teddy snorts out a laugh.

Damn it, Teddy. I was just starting to fall asleep. We're on a flight on our way back from Vancouver and the lull of jet engines always makes me tired. Opening my eyes, I turn to face him. "Dude, it was insane. Great job. But why aren't you sleeping?"

"No way, man. I never sleep on planes."

Maybe he didn't notice that *I* had my eyes shut. I was in the middle of a fantasy I've been having about Cora. In fact, I've been having the same one over and over again for the past three days, since we were out at the post-game party. Yes, the woman's body is insanely gorgeous, but we had fun together. I barely left her side all night long. And fuck if I didn't get hard leaning over her while we played pool. She's all I've been able to think about. She has a wall up made of brick, stone, *and* cinder blocks though.

I'm not sure what I have to do to break the thing down, but I'm willing to give it a shot. She's intrigued me, and I want to find out everything I can about her.

"Too bad, man. I get some of the best sleep I've ever had in the air. But, hey, I was wondering if you noticed that there's a charity auction at Lolita's this weekend. Any interest in going with me?" I put on my cool and collected act, so Teddy can't see how much I want to go.

"You really have a thing for Cora, don't you?" Teddy asks as he runs his fingers through his red hair.

So much for the act. "You can tell?"

"Umm, yeah. You spent all your time with her at the after party. She seems to be a nice girl," he says and then coughs out, "and pretty hot, too."

No kidding. She was attractive in high school, but now she's bikini model sexy with an ass that could win awards. "That's not the only reason I like her. I like what's between her ears; she's level-headed and so damn smart. And it's because she knows me so she isn't star-struck. I can't stand it when women come up to me and pretend to know who I am because they've seen me skate. Cora couldn't care less. It's refreshing."

"It's good to see you happy, man. Especially since the news about Carrie."

Shifting in my seat, I stare him down. "What are you talking about?"

His face goes a shade paler than its already white-ghost like color. "Oh, shit. Haven't you been on the Internet today?"

A sick feeling churns in my stomach. "Just to check my email. You better tell me what the hell is going on."

"Damn. All right. Carrie is in the tabloids with Eddie Carson. They were together at some award show last night." He has a concerned look on his face, like he thinks I might haul off and hit him or something. It's not his damn fault.

I shouldn't care, but hearing it guts me. She was my every-thing and she's already moved on. Our relationship was far from perfect. Her temper would go from zero to one hundred in the blink of an eye. She could go from sweet and comforting to hot and explosive so quickly my head spun. In the same conversation we were embracing, seconds later she'd beat my chest.

Despite her stunning beauty and model-thin body, she's deeply flawed by insecurity. Sent away to boarding school at a young age, her parents never made time for her, their only child. Her mother, an heiress to a health and beauty company, and her father, a self-made millionaire, put work and self-interest before Carrie. You'd think getting paid for your looks would Band-Aid the wounds and give her some sense of self-worth, but it never did.

"This is pissing you off. Let's go to Lolita's and get you a date with Cora." He gives me a conspiratorial grin.

Despite my mood turning to shit seconds ago, the prospect of a date with Cora warms up my insides. One night with her to be alone, catch up, and kiss her again, even if it's just that spot I love near her ear, cheers me a little.

I'm done talking about this with Teddy. "Sounds like a plan. Now leave me alone so I can sleep." Closing my eyes once more, I tilt my head back and let my mind imagine all the things I could do with Cora in one night and let all thoughts of Carrie fall away.

LOLITA'S IS DECKED out for the auction with streamers hanging everywhere and the stage set up with extra lighting and a podium. And it's packed full of horny guys. Tall, short, fat, thin, young, and old, you can smell the testosterone a mile away from the place.

There's no way I'm going to be outbid tonight. None of the

frat boys, motorcycle dudes, juice-heads, or alcoholics in here are going to win against me tonight. The thought of someone else touching her makes me want to find her and throw her over my shoulder.

"Where are all the ladies?" Teddy asks before taking a sip of his pint.

Great question. I've been seeking her out for the past half-hour since we got here. "Maybe they're in the back. What are you going to do? You bidding on anyone?"

"I might bid on Bri. Let's wait and see."

"Why don't you? It's for a good cause, and you like Bri, right?" I ask.

Teddy sighs and turns to face me. "Yeah, she's great, but I don't get the vibe that she's into me."

"Why, because you haven't had sex with her yet?"

He shrugs. "We hung out the other night at the after party, but she seems to have a wall up or something."

"I can relate. So does Cora, but I'll be damned if that stops me from trying." I lean my back against the bar.

"You're more patient than I am," he says and turns back toward the bar to order another drink.

Out of the corner of my eye, I see someone storming toward me. It's Cora in a dick-hardening red dress and tall black boots that come up over her knees. Her shoulders are set back and her head held high like she's going to battle.

"What are you doing here?" she huffs out, as if she's out of breath.

Her mood has caught me off guard; I have no clue how to read her. "Hey, it's nice to see you, too. You look great tonight."

Exhaling through her nose, she says, "I'm sorry, I'm just surprised to see you here."

"The last time I was here I saw the ad for the auction. It's for a good cause, so I thought I'd stop by and bid."

Her hand comes up to her throat and her gaze is trained on me. "Not on me. You aren't here to bid on me." There's panic in her tone. "It's not a good idea."

I grasp the back of her elbow to steady her. She looks like she could use steadying. "What are you afraid of?"

"Nothing. Please, promise me you won't bid on me." Her pupils are fully dilated and she looks like a scared deer standing in headlights seconds before it meets the bumper.

"Okay. You have my word."

Her shoulders relax marginally before she says, "Thank you. I have to go." She strides away from me and doesn't look back.

Confused is an understatement. I wanted to protest and find out the reason she doesn't want me to place a bid, but I couldn't do it. There was something in her tone, her posture. She doesn't want me to bid, so I'm not going to do it.

"You want to go, man? I heard." Teddy swings around, palming his beer.

No, I don't want to go, but what's the sense in staying? "I don't know what to do." I gulp down the rest of my beer.

"Hey, guys." A familiar female voice comes up behind me.

"Bri, hey, how's it going?" Teddy leans in and kisses her on the cheek.

"How are you tonight?" I ask her.

She takes the beer out of Teddy's hand and takes a sip and hands it back to him. "I'm a little nervous about this stupid auction. What if nobody bids on me?"

"You're kidding, right? You look amazing. Everyone is going to try to win a date with you," Teddy says.

She gives him a smile that goes all the way up to her pretty brown eyes. "You think so?"

"Yeah. I'm bidding on you." Teddy nods his head.

"If that's true, I have an idea. How about you bid on Cora," she points at Ted and then at me, "and you bid on me? We can work the rest out later."

"Does this have something to do with the way Cora is acting tonight?" I ask, desperately hoping she can give me some hint as to what's going on in Cora's head.

"Yes. That's exactly it." She glances at her watch. "Damn, I have to go. The auction starts in a minute." She gives us both a conspiratorial smirk and waves as she heads backstage.

And that is just what we do.

The third waitress to take the stage is Cora. She looks stunning, a real-life Barbie doll. But behind her sexy, white-toothed smile, I see what she's trying so hard to hide. She's nervous.

When the bidding begins, Cora's big blue eyes land right on me, sending me a message, imploring me to do what I said I would and not place a bid.

I stuff my hands in my pockets and bite hard on my tongue as bid after filthy bid gets called through the bar. When it seems like it's going to end, I elbow Ted in the ribs and he calls out the final number.

"And the gentleman to my right wins a date with the beautiful Miss Cora," the auctioneer calls out and bangs the lectern with his gavel and it's as if he's beating the thing against my heart. Cora's features relax and she smiles in Teddy's direction and she gives him a wave.

"I won," Teddy says with triumph in his voice.

It should be a relief that he won and not some random asshole in the bar, but it isn't. The nagging in the back of my head won't let me forget how adamant she was that she didn't want it to be me to win the date with her. *Why the hell not?*

"Good for you, man," I say, my tone tense.

"Are you pissed?" He takes one step away from me and looks me up and down.

My posture is stiff. "No. Not at you. At the situation."

"Have a shot or something. We have this under control. Remember the plan."

Before I have a chance to swat Ted or answer back, Bri takes the stage. It's time for me to start bidding.

After a minute of solid back and forth between me and a guy who looks like he swallowed a basketball that landed in his gut, I raise my bid substantially just to get it over with. The big guy shoots me a glare, but it gets the desired result and the bidding ends with me as the winner.

Off to the side of the stage, Cora stands there with her shoulders hunched forward and a bitter smile on her face. Is she upset that I bid on Bri and not her? And if so, why did she ask me—no, beg me—not to bid on her?

I order another beer and take a few calming sips. Teddy is rambling on about how epic it's going to be to pull a switch-a-roo on Cora, but I'm having a hard time staying focused. All I want to do is find Cora and talk to her about everything that happened tonight.

Telling Teddy that I'll be right back, I take off and search for Cora. I look everywhere but can't find her, even going so far as to wait outside the bathroom, but to no avail.

Bri is there talking to Ted when I get back. "Hey, do you know where Cora is?" I ask.

"She took off. I think she went home. Is everything okay?"

Tension rolls off me in waves. Squeezing the back of my neck, I shake my head and say. "No, not really. I'm not doing it, guys. I won't switch dates."

"Why?" Teddy asks.

"Because it's obvious that she doesn't want a date with me. Makes no sense to trick her into it. You can take her out, Ted, since she wants nothing to do with me. I have to get out of here."

They both stare at me open-mouthed and wide-eyed. Before they can say a word, I take my leave and storm out of the bar.

On my way out, a brunette wearing a short skirt grabs me by the arm. "Where are you running off to, handsome? Need some company?"

Yanking my arm away, I give her a hard smile and say, "No, thanks."

It occurs to me that I'm attracted to women who aren't interested in me, but there are so many willing to take me home for a night. It's mind-blowing how little I know about women.

EIGHT

Cora

"WHAT DO YOU HAVE THERE?" my mother asks from her perch on the couch, a tan-colored blanket covering her small legs.

I turn the envelope over again and again. "Not sure. It's from a courier. No return address."

She claps her hands together. "Don't make me wait. Open it already."

I take a seat on the couch next to her. It's sad that the most excitement we've had around here lately is an envelope that gets delivered.

Opening the flap, my stomach clenches when I pull out two tickets to another hockey game. He remembered. But there isn't even a note.

"My gosh, Cora. What is it? You look shaken up."

Breathing deeply, I fill my lungs with air and steady myself. The reaction I've been having to Derek is messing with me. Every touch, every look, every moment I've shared with him has been addicting but it's meant nothing. We aren't dating. Hell, are we even friends? What if I let things progress? It'd only get worse.

That's why I asked him not to bid on me.

It was like a dagger in the heart. He was respecting my wishes, which you'd think would make me happy. Sadly, it didn't.

Thinking of spending an evening with him makes my heart rate speed up. Because would it end at dinner? I doubt it. And I wouldn't want it to. And my God, if I ended up in his bed, I know I'd be a goner.

I stand up and pace back and forth, one end of the living room to the other.

A notch in Derek's bedpost is not something I plan on ever being.

"What's in the envelope, Cora?" Mom asks, concern in her voice.

Steadying my voice, I say, "It's tickets to a hockey game."

With some effort, she sits up straighter. "Who would send you those?"

Faking nonchalance, I sit back down next to her and say, "They're from Derek Parker. Do you remember him?" Wow, even saying his name gives me butterflies. "I tutored him in high school."

"Wasn't he that handsome boy that came by the house a few times? The two of you would sit at the kitchen table and your father would go in there time and time again just to make sure Derek wasn't trying anything with you."

I roll my eyes at the memory. How could I forget? My hard-ass father would walk around the house with his chest puffed out like an orangutan defending my honor. As if Derek was going to try to seduce me or have sex with me on the kitchen table. It was completely unnecessary. My dad was insufferable. "Yes, that was Derek."

"He was a good-looking boy. Why is he sending you hockey tickets?"

"He came into the restaurant. We chatted and he told me how he's in the NHL now. He offered to send me a pair of tickets." No need to add in all the other details. Of course I can't tell her about stripping for him at the bachelor party or the time we were inseparable at the after party. The fewer details she knows, the less ammunition she'll have to try and hook me up with him.

Mom's face brightens into a grin. "Is he married?"

"Very recently divorced," I blurt out, hoping to squash her excitement quickly before it gets out of control.

"Oh, that's too bad. Did you give him your number? Maybe the two of you can catch up soon," she says.

"No, I didn't, Mom. He's a very nice guy, but I'm not attracted to him." Guilt gnaws at me for keeping secrets from her, but it's so much easier than explaining to her the real reasons, like he's a womanizer, and I don't have time for a relationship because I need to take care of her. That, plus I don't want to get my heart broken.

She blinks a few times before she says, "My darling girl. I can see it all over your face. You had a thing for him in high school and things haven't changed now. I don't know what your reasons are for denying your feelings for him, but I know you better than anyone; this boy has gotten to you."

Picking at the corner of the pillow on my lap, I can't look up at her. She's right. I'm terrible at hiding things from her. "Can you trust me? Because I know I wouldn't survive a heart break from him and I'm not about to put myself in a situation where that happens."

"Of course, I trust you. But I'm still going to give you advice. You deserve happiness, so please don't throw it out the window before you give it a chance."

When I look into her eyes, they're full of love and adoration.

"Thanks, Mom. I will always listen to your advice." That's all I can say. No promises.

My mother has always been good at reading me. But how can I let myself get involved with a man like Derek? He was a player and then married a super model.

Would I be just a hook-up? And if that's what he wants, would it be so wrong? Could my heart take it? Could I have sex with him and use him for his body then walk away? If I'm being honest with myself, the answer is no. And he'd never be interested in a relationship with a woman like me, a stripper, college drop-out with a mother that needs to be my top priority.

It's settled. I won't be responding to receiving the tickets with more than a thank you text. But oh, how I'd like to give him more. More gratitude, more of myself. But not now. The timing is all wrong.

"Do you need anything more before I go up and take a shower?" I ask, my thoughts a million miles from here.

She's still, her gaze trained on me with a sympathetic grin. "No, I'm all set here. Love you."

"Love you too, Mom."

"DO you need help cleaning that up?" Bri asks, bringing a bar rag with her.

"No, I've got it," I say from my hands and knees. I've already soaked up most of the mess. An entire tray—five pints of beer—just flew to the floor after I tripped over the air on my way to a table.

Bri comes down on the floor with me and helps get the rest of the mess off the floor. "Everything okay with you today?"

"First of all, I couldn't find the mop, but other than that, I'm fine," I lie. The truth is I've had a hard time focusing for my entire shift today. Getting the hockey tickets yesterday has had me thinking about Derek almost non-stop.

We both stand up at the same time and walk toward the back room to dispose of our beer-drenched towels. "Listen, I can tell that something is off with you today, and I'm here to talk about it when you're ready."

Looking into her warm brown eyes, all I see is patience and kindness and that's all it takes for the floodgates to open. "Maybe I should've let Derek bid on me."

"Why didn't you?" Bri throws the towels in the laundry bag and turns to face me. "You're being stubborn and self-sabotaging. He likes you and you like him. I've seen it every time you're around each other."

"Why sugar coat it? Put it all out there," I say with a laugh.

Her lips form a tight line, but she smiles through it. "Was that harsh?"

Shaking my head, I say, "No. Well, a little, but I needed to hear it. The writing is on the wall. As much as I've been trying to deny it, I'm into him and I'd really like to see where this could go."

Bri jumps up and down, a huge smile plastered on her face. "It's about damn time." She pulls her phone out of her purse and clicks on someone's number. "Damn, he's not picking up. I'm going to leave a message."

"Who is it?" I ask.

She holds up a finger at me to wait and starts talking. "Hey, Derek, it's Bri. Let's set up that date. Call me when you're free."

My pulse starts jumping in my neck at the mention of his name. "What are you doing?" I say, reaching for her phone.

She tucks it back in her pocket. "I, my friend, am doing you a favor and fixing the problem you created by being pig-headed and over-dramatic when you asked Derek not to bid on you." She flings her long wavy brown hair over her shoulder with an "I dare you to disagree" look on her face.

I bite my lower lip to try to stop myself from laughing, but my chest shakes, and I can't help myself. A belly giggle bubbles up from deep inside as if all the hiding and pushing down my feelings is finally being let out because I admitted them to Bri.

"What's so funny?" She gives me a puzzled stare.

Reaching out, I hold onto the wall for stability to get through my laughing fit. Winded, I finally say, "Nothing is funny; it just feels really good to laugh. Now tell me, what's your plan?"

Bri takes me by the arm and leads me out of the back room while she fills me in on her plan.

* * *

THE ITALIAN RESTAURANT IS SWANKY, from the white chair covers to the crystal chandeliers. It's as if I'm attending someone's wedding, not a set-up date where the person I'm meeting doesn't even know it's me who's coming. Poor Derek. We've most definitely set him up.

A tall thin man with a white shirt and black bow tie leads me back to Derek's table.

The temperature of the room goes up at least fifty degrees when Derek's eyes lock on mine. His smile widens, and he scans my body. It looks as though he likes what I'm wearing. It's a red V-neck cocktail dress, showing only a tasteful amount of cleavage. When I heard where Derek made the reservation, I knew I couldn't wear any old dress and certainly nothing I'd wear for one of my jobs.

Derek is up, out of his chair, and standing in front of me. A shiver moves through me as I watch Derek drink me in. I do the same, taking in his sex-on-a-stick body, dressed in a perfectly tailored three-piece suit. I'm realizing now what a turn-on a well-dressed man is for me, especially since that's typically what I see Derek wearing.

There's a charge in the air between us. I'm certain that if I put my hand up, I could feel it sizzling through my fingers.

"You're here," he says, almost as if he isn't surprised to see me, like he bid on me and expected me here tonight instead of Bri.

"Did you know I was coming?"

"I hoped it'd be you." He flashes me a heart-stopping grin.

My knees weaken. "Is it okay if we sit?"

"Of course." He pivots, pulls a chair out for me, and takes his seat across from mine. "Thank you for coming. You know it was you I wanted to bid on at the auction, right?"

Looking down at my hands, I take a moment before I speak. He deserves an answer, not because of the insane amount of money he spent on this date, but because he seems interested in me and if there's a prayer in hell this could go somewhere, I have to talk to him. I look up at his beautiful face before I say, "I'm sorry about that."

His gaze holds mine. "Don't apologize. Clearly, it worked out since you're here and Bri's not, but I am curious why you asked me not to bid on you."

A waiter stops by the table with a bottle of red wine and pours us each a glass. Derek nods at him and the waiter walks away. "I hope you don't mind. I took the liberty of ordering. If it isn't to your liking we can get something else."

Grateful for the courage in a glass, I tap mine with his and take a swallow. "No, this is delicious. Thank you. And about the other night..." I clear my throat. "It's complicated."

He nods, studying me, his dark eyes piercing like he's trying to see through me.

I've prepared myself for this, carefully planning out how this conversation would go. Yet here I am at a loss for words. Every time I'm with Derek, he throws me off balance. "The truth is you make me nervous." There, I said it.

He lets out a harsh laugh. "Shit, sorry. I didn't mean to laugh." Taking a moment to collect himself, he puts his hand over his mouth. "It was funny because we're both on the same page. I didn't expect you to say it though."

Relief washes over me. He's scared, too. "What scares you?"

The waiter stops by and drops off two plates, one with calamari and the other crostini with some type of cheese and red sauce over it. My mouth waters. Derek thanks the waiter and he walks away.

"I don't know if you know anything about my divorce. Unfortunately, it's been pretty public," he says quietly.

"Not much. I heard you were married to Carrie White and recently got divorced," I tell him, keeping my eyes on the food.

He sits up straighter. "Talking about this isn't easy for me, but you asked what scares me, so here it is. I loved Carrie. She was it for me and I thought we were going to grow old together. Apparently, the same wasn't true for her. Things got ugly toward the end. She hated it when I had to travel, which with my career I have to do. Carrie liked to pick fights with me, sometimes in public." Turning his head to the side, the muscles in his jaw tic. "She picked a fight with me at a movie premiere. She said I was flirting with someone and started hitting me in the chest. It wasn't true. Jealousy became her dominant emotion. She's a model and gets paid for her looks, yet she's deeply insecure. Things didn't end well."

This is all new information to me. Of course, I Googled his ex. She's an absolutely stunning woman, long straight dark hair, a thin tight body, and soft features. Being beautiful on the outside doesn't mean you aren't flawed on the inside. "Oh, wow. I didn't know that. I'm sorry."

"No, you don't have to apologize. The reason I'm telling you is because I don't often feel this way about women, and the last time I did, it didn't end well. When you came back into my life I wasn't looking for another woman, but you intrigue me, Cora." His gaze is full of heat and desire.

My heart rate quickens. What can he possibly see in me?

Derek takes a piece of the bread and sets it on his plate. "Tell me what scares you about me."

Tapping my foot against the floor, I lift my fork and take a few pieces of calamari for my plate, simply for something to do with my hands. I set the fork down and wipe my clammy palms on my dress. "In high school, I had a crush on you. I'm sure you already knew that. And seeing you again proved to me that there's still something there."

"If you feel that way, why would you tell me not to bid on you? Why not give us a chance?" His expression is bleak and his brows knit together.

"What do you see in me, Derek? I'm a stripper. I don't have anything to offer you," I snap with an edge to my tone.

"Nope." He holds up a finger. "First of all, your job doesn't define you. At all. You're so much more than that. You're smart and funny, not to mention gorgeous. But don't do that. Don't change the subject."

My jaw goes slack. I didn't know he felt that way about me. "My mom is sick. She has a progressive form of MS. Dad died five years ago. I'm the only one left to take care of her. I quit school and came home. That's why I work at Lolita's and do stri-pagrams. I don't like the work, but it pays the bills."

He reaches across the table and takes my hand in his. It's big and warm, comforting me immediately and easing the ache that was in my chest. "Shit. I had no idea. I'm sorry to hear about your father. And Adeline is a sweetheart; it's terrible that she's sick."

"Thank you. You're right; it's awful watching her lose her strength and independence. It isn't a lie when I tell you that I'm busy. All the time. If I don't work, we can't afford my mom's care. That's why I was hesitant to come out on a date with you. I'm not an easy person to date since my time is limited."

Derek lets go of my hand and I instantly miss it. "We're both busy people, Cora. That's not an excuse. There has to be more to it." There they are again, his probing eyes that seem to bore through me.

I drink the last bit of wine in my glass and set it in front of me. "I take dating very seriously. Or at least I used to, but I haven't had much luck. Now I find it difficult to take time for men who only want me for one reason."

Derek sucks in a sharp breath. "Are you saying men try to use you for sex?"

Hanging my head, I wipe my hands across my face before I look back up. "Why would I expect anything different? They see me at work, or hear what my job is, so naturally they think I'm easy. But I'm not." My voice rises.

He pours us each another glass of wine and takes a large mouthful of his. "I can't tell you how infuriated I am that people treat you that way. Just because you work at Lolita's doesn't mean you're a slut."

"Exactly, but apparently most guys think that. I don't bother anymore—it's a waste of time that I don't have." I take a bite of the calamari, which is incredible. Right now food seems like an excellent distraction.

"No wonder you don't date. But I can assure you that isn't why I wanted to take you out. You just admitted that you had a crush on me and the feeling is mutual. What do you say we go out on another date?"

How can I say no, even when my sensibilities tell me not to? Would another date really be so bad? He's sitting here in front of me, vulnerable and opening up about his ex. Hell, I couldn't say no if I tried. "Sure, let's do it."

His face brightens into a smile. "Yes! Let's go dancing or something. Don't worry, I'll plan it. We could even stay in and watch a movie with your mom. Doesn't matter. I just want to hang out with you."

I can't help myself and grin from ear to ear. "Sounds great."

The waiter brings out several plates of filet, seafood, and salad.

"I took the liberty of ordering the full meal. I hope you like it." He smirks.

Something tells me that Derek is a man who likes to take liberties in every aspect of his life.

NINE

Derek

THE WRAPPER on the flowers rattles. My hands are shaking like I'm in the final playoff game to take home the Stanley Cup.

I knock on her apartment door and shove my hand through my hair. *Get your shit together; it's going to be fine. Her mom's going to like you.*

I'll be damned.

Cora swings open the door. She looks good enough to eat in her black leggings and blue sweater that hugs her curves mouth-wateringly well. Her face is glowing and it doesn't look like she has on a stitch of makeup. A natural fucking beauty.

Close your mouth. Wipe off the drool.

"Hi." She gives me a shy smile as she takes the flowers. "They're beautiful. Come in."

The house hasn't changed from what I remember of it. There were a few occasions when our tutoring sessions took place right here in this kitchen. A flood of memories come back of Cora patiently teaching me what I wasn't picking up from our teacher at school. She deserved more than what my parents paid her. I never would've passed without her.

The furnishings are updated, but the warm, homey feeling is the same. "Thanks for inviting me."

"My mom's excited to see you. Let's go in the living room." She leads the way and I can't take my eyes off her perfect ass. Shame on me for having such inappropriate thoughts seconds before I see her mother.

I haven't been able to stop thinking about her since our date last week. Now that I know the true reason for her taking on the job at Lolita's as well as the side stripping jobs, it all makes sense. It doesn't make it any easier to swallow though. I hate the thought of her taking off her clothes for men, but I have no right to tell her not to, or to judge her.

Damn. Her mother is sitting up in a chair, face gaunt and pale. She's lost weight, and she wasn't a big woman to begin with. There's a walker next to her chair. Even fully clothed, I can tell the muscles of her legs have atrophied. Despite all of that, her face comes alive with a warm smile when she sees me.

Cora stands behind her mother's chair and she squeezes her shoulders , giving her a little massage. "Mom, you remember Derek, right?"

"Derek Parker, it's lovely to see you. Come over here and give me a hug."

Striding across the room, I'm in front of her and wrapping her up in my arms. She's nothing but skin and bones. My heart aches for her and for Cora. I know it isn't easy for her to see her mother get sicker and weaker.

I pull away and say, "It's good to see you, Adeline. Thanks for having me over."

"Glad to have you. When Cora told me that the two of you

met up again, I couldn't be happier." She claps her hands in front of her.

Cora walks to the couch to sit down and gives her mom a warning look, but she still has a smile on her face. "Now let's not go giving too many of our secrets away, okay, Mom?"

My heart swells watching the two of them together. They were always close. I remember seeing the two of them out taking walks together on the trail I used to run on back in school. Adeline and Cora would often be making dinner or baking together when I came over for my tutoring sessions. And hearing their playful banter now, it seems that hasn't changed. "I'm with you, Adeline. It's been great getting to know Cora again. And you can give away as many secrets as you'd like."

Adeline chuckles. "Let's just say my daughter doesn't bring men around for me to meet. For a while I thought she made the decision to live a life of celibacy."

I take a seat on the couch next to Cora and bite my lip to stifle a laugh.

"Okay, should we start the movie now?" Cora quickly says and clicks the buttons on the remote to play the movie.

It's a chick flick, not normally my type of film. I'm more of an action adventure kind of guy, but I'd watch anything to sit this close to Cora. She got up and brought two plates of cheese and crackers, handing one to her mother and setting the other on the ottoman in front of us. I pop a piece of cheese in my mouth and move in closer to her.

At first our thighs graze each other, the heat from her leg instantly transferring to mine, shooting adrenaline straight through me. It's not enough contact. I want more but I'm going to stay on my best behavior. I told her that I wasn't like the other guys who want to use her for sex. And I'm not that guy. But what if I hold her hand? That wouldn't be too much, would it? Fuck it.

Twining her fingers through mine, I grasp her small hand, encasing it in mine. My god it feels good.

Cora looks down at our hands joined together and then up at me. She bites her bottom lip and looks back at the television.

Neither of us moves for the rest of the movie. Still as stone, with the exception of my thumb running over her knuckles or her nails gliding over my palm. It's a simple act, but it's erotic and intimate and unsafe.

By the end of the movie, Adeline is asleep in her chair. Cora wakes her and helps her to bed after I give her a goodbye hug.

Waiting in the living room for Cora gives me a chance to reflect on the evening. My heart swells seeing the love and commitment between Cora and her mother. I want to help them. I wish I knew how.

And then there's the lust. The real, undeniable pull toward Cora. My body craves contact with hers. While holding hands was great, I want more.

She comes back in the living room as if she's apprehensive. She takes her spot on the couch, but puts too much space between us.

We both start to speak at the same time and both uncomfortably giggle at the same time. "You go first," Cora says.

"About your mother." Planning to talk about Adeline and possibly helping out with her medical care or how I can help might take my mind off how much I want to touch her.

"No. I mean, let's not talk about her now," she says, shifting her body toward me.

"What do you want to talk about?" I rest my arm along the back of the couch, my fingers close enough to touch her shoulder, but I don't.

"Us. I need to get some things off my chest. I've been thinking about this all night. Maybe longer." She straightens her shoulders and there's a tight set to her jaw.

Now I really want to rub her shoulders. Whatever she has to say is causing her a great deal of tension. "Okay, I'm all ears."

"I want to kiss you and so much more than that. And I don't know what that means. For me or for you. It's stressing me out because I haven't felt this way in a long time and I don't know what I can offer you, Derek. I won't be an easy girlfriend to have because I don't have free time and my mother is my number one priority." Her chest rises and falls on a deep breath and she inches herself closer to me. "If that means we're just casual, I'm going to have to be okay with that. I mean, if you are." Her words come out in a tumble and she looks so damn beautiful and vulnerable.

Leaning in closer to her, I rest my forehead against hers and cup her cool cheeks in my hands. Her breath is shaky, like mine, but she told me she wants to kiss me and I'm not going to let her down.

It's gentle at first, only her soft full lips against mine. She smells like roses in full bloom on a hot summer day and she tastes sweet, exactly like I dreamed she'd be. My tongue is greedy and presses against hers in a perfect rhythm. A moan escapes her lips and my cock hardens. I put one of my hands through her silky blonde hair, moving to the back of her head and pushing her mouth closer to me, deepening the kiss. It's escalating fast, the pressure, the speed, the intensity. All of it.

I want to devour her. Every inch. But not if she's not ready.

Pulling back, we both catch our breaths, staring into each other's eyes. "Is this too much too soon?" I ask.

"I'm scared." Her voice is low and throaty.

"I don't want to hurt you, Cora. We go at your pace." From deep inside me, I mean this. All I want is to make her happy.

She nods with half-lidded eyes. "My pace."

"Yes. What do you want tonight? Don't overthink it."

"I want you." She stands and gives me the come here gesture

with her index finger. Taking me toward the back of the house, she leads me to her bedroom. If I thought I was horny before, it's cranked up one hundredfold now. *Take it easy. You will not rush this.*

When I close the door behind us, I can't wait another second to get my hands on her. I walk up to her and guide her backward to her bed until it hits the back of her knees and she falls back onto it. Her blonde hair glows all around her like she's an angel.

"Tell me if I go too fast. I'll stop if you want me to," I say.

She nods. "Okay."

I tug my shirt off and toss it to the floor. Her eyes scan my chest and abs, a look of complete admiration on her face. Glad she likes my six pack. I've always prided myself on my work ethic in all aspects of my life and that includes the gym.

I lean over her and lift the blue sweater over her head and reach around and unhook her black silk bra, sending it to land with the other clothes.

Sitting back, I'm in awe of this woman. This smart, loyal, hotter than hell woman is lying in front of me. I almost pinch myself, but instead, I admire her full, round breasts. I play with her nipple until it stiffens to a hard point under my fingers. "You're absolutely fucking gorgeous."

"So are you." Her voice is throaty and sexy as hell.

Enough of these damn clothes. I take off my jeans and boxer briefs and get to work on her leggings, stripping them off one leg at a time. All that's left is a tiny black lace thong that I nearly rip off. *Patience, Derek.*

Raking my eyes over her naked body, she shivers like she's self-conscious. No way. There's no reason this stunningly beautiful woman should ever feel insecure. I'm going to make it my job to show her now just how much I think of her.

I kiss my way up her flat stomach and take her nipple in my mouth, licking and sucking. So sweet, I savor it like candy. The noises coming out of her mouth, desperate throaty moans, make me nearly go before we even get started. Not this time. I have to be inside her with her naked body pressed against mine.

Easing my way up her, I press my lips to my favorite spot next to her ear and lick the tender flesh, sucking it in, but not hard enough to leave a mark. She tastes so damn good and addictive.

Drawing in a deep breath, Cora says, "My god, Derek. I don't think I can wait. Reach in my nightstand drawer. I've got condoms."

Damn, she's as impatient as I am. She doesn't have to ask twice. I put my weight on one arm and open the drawer with the other and find a condom. Ripping it open with my teeth and rolling it on, I ease back over her.

The head of my dick rests right at her entrance and I rub it over her clit again and again teasing her, and myself.

Cora's eyes are squeezed shut and she tilts her hips up, needing me inside her. I know how she feels. I need it, too.

"You're so wet," I hiss out and ease myself in slowly.

Our eyes lock as I sink in, inch by inch. "You feel so good, Derek."

"So fucking good."

Our mouths crash together, all of our lust and desire finally coming to fruition. Digging my fingers into her soft round hips, I plunge in as far as I can go. Her nails scrape down my back and my head starts spinning. My pace picks up so she wraps her legs around my waist.

Please let me keep it together.

Her smell surrounds me, her smooth flesh glides against mine, and our breathing is in sync. *We* are in sync. This connection is deeper than sex; I can see it in her eyes and hear it in the soft murmurs escaping her lips.

She is everything.

This is everything.

"Oh, Derek. Please don't stop," Cora moans into my ear as her legs and arms tense around me.

No way in hell. Pushing up, I take both her legs in my hands and angle them back, giving me more leverage. Cora grabs for her ankles and I thrust in and out. My breathing gets erratic and I know I'm close.

Reaching down with one hand, I massage her clit, soft and even with the drive of my hips.

Cora's blue eyes roll back in her head, her breathing gets hard, and her chest heaves. "Yes."

Seconds later, her entire body jerks and shudders.

It's nothing short of earth-shattering when I join her and go with a long satisfying groan.

Lying down next to her, I pull her onto me, chest to chest. I stroke her hair and love the feel of her warm breath on me. This is heaven. Heat swells up in me and I don't know what to make of all of this. The air is thick with the unknown, but right now I'm going to enjoy this.

"Think we woke up your mother?" I ask.

Her half-lidded blue eyes look up into mine. "No, she's at the other end of the house."

"Good, because that time was fast and primal. In a few minutes I want to do slow and romantic."

This perks her up and she puts her hand under her chin. "Oh, really?"

"Really. I had plans. We would take our time and draw it out, but instead, you drove me crazy. I almost went simply by touching you."

She giggles. "Sorry I ruined your plans."

Pulling her up to face me, I plant a kiss on her mouth. "Oh, no. Nothing was ruined. It was fucking perfect."

Her brows knit together and her lips form a tight line. "Do you want to talk about us now? Because I think we should."

"If there's something on your mind, let's talk," I say and sweep circles on her back with my fingertip. A small attempt to relax her.

"You scare me, Derek. I'm afraid you're going to hurt me. I have to know where you stand so I can protect myself. Because if this is only about sex for you, that's fine. I just need to know." Her tone is clipped and she isn't making eye contact.

I lift her chin so she'll look at me. "What do you want?" She's all over the place, and I'm no good at guessing games.

A tear forms in the corner of her eye, but she blinks and wipes at it. "I don't know, and I'm sorry if I'm confusing you, but I do know I like being around you. We always have fun when we're together."

"Agreed. Would it be okay if we started with spending time together? No labels or preconceived notions? Would that scare you?" I ask. Because the reality is that I'm not sure what kind of boyfriend I'd be. Giving my everything to Carrie and having her rip it all away took a major toll on me. Am I ready to move on and start over? I know one thing: I want Cora in my life in some capacity.

"No. I don't think so. I mean, I don't know." She lets out a heavy sigh and lays her head back on my chest, her long, blonde, just had sex hair tickling my skin.

"How about this? Let's stop pretending that we don't want to be together. In a perfect world, all of this would be easy, but nothing good ever is easy, right?" I say.

Shifting her position, she lies on her side, body perpendicular to mine. Her eyes sparkle and gleam. "I guess not. Let's not talk anymore." Her lips come to mine and that's all the talking we do for the rest of the night.

TEN

Cora

"CHEERS TO TONIGHT," Bri says and we both take a sip of the dark liquid at the bar.

"Thanks for meeting me. I needed a little liquid courage before we meet up with everyone else," I say. A slew of butterflies erupt in my belly. I still can't believe that Bri and I are meeting Derek, Teddy, Rick and his fiancée, Rose, and Wes and his girlfriend, the country music star, Lydia Crow, for dinner here tonight.

"Why are you nervous?" Bri adjusts the top of her dress. It's a strapless floral number that highlights her small but toned shoulders. Her long brown hair is swept back in a low ponytail, giving her an elegant, sophisticated look.

"It's not every day that we get a chance to eat dinner here with part of the Nashville Wolverines hockey team."

Bri looks around the restaurant. I know she's admiring the contemporary exposed ceilings and décor. It's all farmhouse-style solid wood tables and metal chairs. It has a long bar spanning one wall with a huge collection of wine, liquor, and beer. The kitchen is open with a massive brick oven in the center. It's known for having all homemade, fresh, organic ingredients, with everything made to order. And it costs a pretty penny. It has a five fork review in the *Times* when it first opened last year and the waiting list to get a reservation is months long, unless you know someone, like an NHL player or a popular country music singer.

"Don't worry. It's going to be a great time," Bri says as she fiddles with her beaded necklace. "I'm sorry, I can't hold it in anymore, I have to tell you."

"What is it?"

She takes a long swallow of her wine and sets it in front of her. "Okay. I took my exam to get my real estate license and I just found out I passed. I'm going to start applying for jobs. I'm giving Steve my notice as soon as I get hired."

Throwing my arms around her, I say, "Congratulations. I'm so happy for you. I know how long you've wanted to do this."

"You aren't mad at me?" Even though Bri is excited, she has a frown on her face.

There's a tiny slice of me that's envious of her for getting out of Lolita's and moving on to do what she's always wanted to do with her life, but I'm thrilled for her. "I'm going to miss you when you leave, but you deserve this."

A huge grin spreads across her face. "Thank you. Tommy was never supportive of my dreams. As soon as the divorce was finalized, I got the information to work toward getting my license."

"Good for you," I say and give her shoulder a squeeze.

"What about you and Derek? How are you two doing?"

Heat creeps up my cheeks thinking about last night. Derek kept me up most of the night making love. He has skills in the bedroom that I've never experienced before, not to mention the intimacy we shared. It was a night I won't soon forget. "Things have been good."

Bri caught my look. "No way. You aren't getting out of it that easy. Did you two have sex?"

"Things did heat up between us last night." I'm being coy. It's too much fun to tease Bri.

"And?"

"We did it and it was ah-freaking-mazing," I squeal.

Bri shrieks and bounces up and down on her toes, grabbing me by the arm. "Holy shit. You're actually glowing. It must've been dreamy."

"It was. Every minute. He's powerful and strong, and at the same time gentle and sweet. He took care of me in every way." I suck in a breath. My heart beat speeds up at the memory of Derek's hands sliding down my body, his dark eyes searing through me with such passion and intensity.

"Why do you look like that?" Bri asks.

"What do you mean?"

She narrows her eyes at me. "You're telling me that you had great sex, but your face turned pale. Are you scared or something?"

"Of course I am. I feel like I'm falling so hard for him that I'm going to land face first on the concrete," I huff out a laugh.

"Get out of your damn head," Bri pronounces with a point to her head. "Can you try to have fun for once?"

Easier said than done. "I want to. When I'm with Derek, I'm happy and I do want to relax and enjoy the ride. I'm going to try. Ok."

"Good," Bri says.

"What about you and Teddy?"

She gets her lip gloss out of her purse and applies a thin coat. "He's sweet and we have fun when we hang out, but he's not the settle down type. At all. He's a great friend though, and when we're together there's no pressure."

"No sex?" The last couple times I've seen them together, they seem to have chemistry.

"He's a ladies' man and I have no interest in being another one of his conquests," Bri says and tries her cabernet.

Crossing my legs, I smooth down my navy dress. "I can relate. Here's some of your own advice. Why don't you take it day by day?"

Teddy sneaks up behind Bri and puts his finger over his lips, signaling me to not give him away. He snakes his arm around Bri and kisses her cheek. Bri's face breaks out in a blush.

Sure they're just friends.

Derek follows after Teddy and comes up to me and gives me a kiss square on the lips. No tongue, but it doesn't matter; it still gets me excited. "You look stunning tonight, Cora."

My eyes drink in Derek in his charcoal gray pants, white button up shirt, and navy silk tie. "You're not so shabby yourself. We match." I grab hold of his tie and pull him closer for another kiss.

"We must be on the same wavelength." He winks and grabs my hand. "Come on, our table is ready."

I follow him to the back of the restaurant, where our table is tucked into a secluded corner. Teddy and Bri follow behind.

Wes, Derek's best friend, who is dating the ultra-famous Lydia Crow are already seated and there's a tall, bulky man I can only assume is a bodyguard standing stock straight against the wall closest to Lydia. Seeing her sitting there, I'm a bit star struck . She's even more beautiful in person, with long straight blonde hair and almost shocking gray-blue eyes.

At the table, Wes and Lydia stand to greet us. "Hey, buddy." Wes shakes Derek's hand and takes mine. "Nice to see you again.

This is my girlfriend, Lydia." Derek hugs her and she gives me a hug, too.

Turning around, Bri's mouth is wide open, clearly in awe of Lydia, too.

Rick introduces us to his fiancée, Rose. Her hair is brown, cut into a sleek bob and she has piercing green eyes. She's sitting across the table and gives Bri and me a wave.

We sit down and order drinks and appetizers. I have Derek on one side of me and Bri on the other. The conversation flows and I'm oddly at ease with this group. Maybe it's the drinks I had at the bar with Bri, or it could be that this is just a great group of people.

"Aren't Rick and Rose cute together?" Bri whispers in my ear.

"Adorable." They finish each other's sentences and they're always sharing a look or a touch.

The waitress delivers oysters, huge shrimp cocktail, bruschetta bread, and escargot to the table. "Can I take your meal order now?" she asks.

"Sure," Rose says, clasping the menu in her hand. "He will have the large filet with béarnaise sauce, cooked medium rare, with a side of sweet potato puree. And I will have the sea bass."

"Are you kidding me?" Teddy chuckles. "Rose orders your food for you?"

"You want to start taking digs at each other? Because I can go there if you want to." Rick has a menacing smirk on his face.

Teddy holds his hands up. "Nope. I'm good."

Everyone at the table laughs. From the short amount of time I've spent around the guys, Teddy seems to get himself into funny situations that make him the brunt of most of their jokes.

We all place our orders and Derek kisses my cheek. He leans in close to my ear and his clean masculine scent warms me from the inside. Kissing the sensitive skin next to my ear heats me up even more. "I enjoyed myself at your house. I can't wait to do it again. Can you come to my place after dinner?"

What I wouldn't give to go to his place and get intimate with him again. I turn toward him, his proximity throwing me off. We're breathing the same air and it makes me want to leave here now. "Sadly, I don't have anyone to check in on Mom tonight. I don't like to leave her overnight without someone nearby. I wish I could though."

"It isn't safe for her to stay alone, is it?" Concern creases his dark brows.

"No. I worry that she'll get up in the middle of the night to use the bathroom or need me." I get a sick feeling in my gut at the memory of my mother falling out of bed a few months ago. She was frightened but didn't want to wake me, so she lay on the floor all night. I scolded her for not getting me up to help her.

Derek's hand grasps my thigh. "Is there anything I can do to help?"

"No, I can take care of her."

"I know you can, but she might be more comfortable in an assisted living home or with a full-time nurse. My uncle sits on the board at Riverview. I could make a call."

Riverview is an expensive assisted living home that has a waiting list a mile long to get a room. One of Mom's doctors told us that that was where she'd want to be when the time came. Of course, neither she nor I are ready for that yet. "I can't do that. She wants to be at home." There's an edge to my tone.

He gives my thigh a comforting squeeze. "I'm sorry. I didn't mean to upset you. Your mother is a sweet woman. I only wanted to help out."

Taking a few calming breaths, I relax myself. Derek is well-intended even if his idea is ridiculous because it's so unaffordable. "I know. I'm sorry. And about your invite, can I get a rain check?"

"Of course," Derek says and smiles before popping a shrimp into his mouth.

The meal proceeds and I watch everyone at the table. There's friendship and laughter, but there's also prestige and money, two things I don't have. Even now Bri has her dream job and here I sit, still a stripper. I don't think the women I met tonight have any idea where I work or that I met the guys stripping at Rick's bachelor party, but deep down I feel like I don't fit in.

"I need to use the restroom. I'll be right back," I tell Derek as I get up from the table.

Rose is washing her hands when I get in the bathroom. "Cora, I'm glad you're here." She shuts off the water and grabs a paper towel. "I know we don't know each other well yet, but I'm pretty good at reading people."

"Oh," I say because I can't think of anything better to say. My curiosity is piqued.

"Yes. I like you. And Rick told me that Derek is smitten with you, and boy can I see it." Her smile widens. "He's been miserable and hard to deal with since Carrie broke his heart, according to the guys. Now he seems better."

My jaw hangs open. "We just started dating, if that's what we're even calling it."

"What's your hesitation?" She leans her hip against the vanity.

"I don't want to get hurt." My voice comes out pathetic and small.

Rose gets closer and grasps my arms. "Oh, honey, isn't that life? There are no guarantees, but when Derek settles down, you won't have anything to worry about. I saw the way he looks at you. There's something there. I see it between you."

I'm caught off guard. When Derek and I are together, I feel the chemistry, but to have someone else tell me that they see it, that's entirely something else. "Thank you."

"Of course. The guys on the team are like family, and Rick and Derek are close. They like to see each other happy. Do you have your phone with you?"

"Yes." I pull it out of my purse.

"Here's my number, text me yours. We can get together soon."

"I'd like that," I say and give her a genuine smile. It warms my heart that this woman who barely knows me seems to be welcoming me to the group.

Back at the table, everyone is talking about one of the other players named Marcus.

"He keeps bragging in the locker room about screwing a nineteen-year-old. Like we'd be impressed that he's cheating on Alex," Teddy says, his face twisted in disgust.

"We should tell Alex. I'd want to know if I were her," Rose chimes in. I like her more by the minute.

Teddy takes a piece of bruschetta off the platter and sets it on the plate, licking the tomato juice off his fingers. "It's not a good idea. We barely know Alex. What if they have an open relationship?"

Lydia pipes up, "I doubt that."

"The problem is that you never know if Marcus is lying or not. He's an asshole. Until we have proof, I don't think any of us should get in the middle of it," Rick points out.

Rose rolls her eyes and shakes her head. "He's such a dick. I'm glad you guys don't hang out with him." She takes a sip of her martini and sets it in front of her. "How did he end up with Alex anyway? She's a doctor, so we know she's smart, and she seemed sweet when we talked at the last after party. I can't understand why she's with him."

"He's a smooth talker. Chicks dig that," Rick says, refilling his wine glass.

"Not me," I say.

Derek squeezes my thigh and heat moves up my leg. He whispers in my ear, his warm breath heating the lobe. "Don't worry, I'm not an asshole like Marcus."

Deep inside, I know he's telling me the truth.

Oh, how I wish I could go home with him tonight.

ELEVEN

Derek

I CRACK OPEN a beer after unpacking and sink into my couch. It's been a long four days away. Three games in as many cities. It's good to be home.

I've missed Cora. She's slowly starting to become an addiction. When she's not around, I crave her. It'd be nice to see her tonight, but she has to work and I need to relax.

Cora's been nervous about us, but I've been doing my damnedest to show her she can trust me. In the process, I think I could be falling for her. Fuck if it doesn't scare me, but it feels so good.

In the last month, I've taken her out and wined and dined her. When I'm out of town, we talk and text a few times a day. She's spent the night at my place twice now. It's not enough, but I take whatever she gives me.

I'm breaking through her barriers. She seems to be loosening up more every day, opening up more and more, and in turn so am

I. It's unreal how easy it is to be around her. She feels like home to me, more than Carrie ever did.

There's only one problem. As the days go by, I'm feeling more and more possessive of her. But I know if I push her too hard to quit her job or take my offer to help her out with her mother, she'll push back. Cora is nothing if not stubborn. It's okay though. For now. I can give her time. She's worth it.

There's a knock at my door. I'm not expecting anyone tonight. It has to be Cora surprising me. A huge smile spreads across my face.

Getting up, I walk to the door and swing it open.

You've got to be kidding me.

"Hey, handsome." Carrie leans against the doorframe, one leg crossed over the other, as casual as ever. Her silky blonde hair is pin-straight; she has it all swept over one shoulder.

Old, unresolved feelings come flooding back. The attraction is still there, but now there's an undercurrent of hurt, bitterness, and resentment. "What are you doing here?"

Carrie has her arms around me and for a minute, smelling her jasmine perfume, I'm taken back to the good times and the love.

But I'm not stupid.

I pull away. "What do you need, Carrie?"

"I miss you and wanted to see you." She's wearing the sexy smile that used to get to me all the time. Fuck, is she trying to seduce me?

"What does that mean?" I huff out.

"Can I come in?" she asks.

I close the door behind her and we go to the living room. Neither of us sits down. She stands too close to me.

She lays her hands on my chest. I wonder if she can feel the way my heart beats around her. It used to go crazy, thundering against my chest when she walked in the room. Now it sits there, crushed after the shit she put me through. "It's been a long time," she says.

With a sigh, I look down at her hands and remove them. "Right, but I saw online that you've been keeping yourself very busy." I try unsuccessfully to keep the edge out of my tone.

"Oh, you're talking about the pictures of me and Eddie. That's nothing." She rolls her eyes and waves her hand in the air.

"Looked like something to me," I say.

"What about you? Who's the girl you've been photographed with? I didn't like seeing you with someone else." She crosses her arms in front of her chest and pouts.

Irritation prickles the back of my neck. Where does she get off asking me anything? She lost that right when she filed the divorce papers. "You think I liked it? Seeing you with someone else? I didn't."

She sits down on the couch and pats the spot next to her. "Why don't we try again? I want you back."

I stay standing, needing to keep my distance and my wits about me. Here she is offering me everything I've wanted for so long. Of course I'm tempted. I loved her so much. But this isn't real. "It's because you're jealous. Nothing else has changed. I'm still going to have to travel."

Carrie stands in front of me again, studying me. "I've changed, Derek. I know what I want and it's you." Her hand comes up and rubs against my dick.

I don't get hard.

Before that's all it took, a glance, a graze, her breath on my skin. Not today.

"Tell me you don't miss me." She tries unzipping my jeans.

Grasping her hand in mine, I push it away. "Stop," I growl.

Her lip quivers. "It's her, isn't it? The woman in the pictures. You care for her. Do you love her?"

Do I? I'm not sure if what I'm feeling is love or not. I care for

Cora. And it's been impossible not to think about her every day when I wake up and go to sleep. Christ, she's even made very vivid appearances in my dreams. It's intense, but am I in love? "You know this is none of your business now. You left me, remember?"

She starts crying, big ugly tears. Does it make me a cold heartless bastard if I don't care? Walking into the bathroom, I get the box of tissues and bring them out to her. "Carrie, I'm sorry that you're hurting, but I think you should go."

She wipes her cheeks, smearing black mascara all over. "Please don't push me away. I want to try again."

How many times had I said those exact same words while *she* pushed me away? Again and again. Ironic since I'm finally over her. Today solidified it. "You should go now." I walk toward the door and open it for her.

Anger flashes across her face, the same look she used to get before she'd haul off and slap me across the face. She reapplies her heartless mask, sets her shoulders back, and flips me off before she walks out the door.

I made the right decision.

IT'S GAME DAY. I slept like a baby last night after Carrie left. Now that I know I'm completely over her, it's like a giant burden has been lifted.

Warm-ups are finishing up now. I hammer one last shot at the net and skate off to the bench.

Looking up into the stands, I see Cora made it. She notices me and her lips curve into a bright smile. Happiness washes over me.

Slick nudges me in my side. "No shit. You invited Carrie."

My head snaps to his. "What?"

Pointing up, he says, "Over there."

Damn it. She's sitting a few seats over from Cora. "What the hell is she doing here?"

"You didn't tell her to come?" Slick says, hurling himself over the boards and onto the bench.

"No. I didn't." She better not be here to talk to Cora. I grip my stick harder than necessary and take the ice.

This might be my worst game this season. I'm distracted the entire game. Cora left a few minutes after the third period started and she looked like she was in a hurry. Thinking that Carrie told Cora something, I couldn't stay focused. I missed shots I should've made and had three penalties.

No thanks to me, we win the game. Teddy had some great saves tonight.

Back in the locker room, I get my cell phone out and call Cora.

I almost throw the phone across the room when she doesn't answer but think better of it.

Now I'm worried.

TWELVE

Cora

"DRIVE FASTER!" I scream at the Uber driver. My heart races and tears fall down my cheeks.

Why did I come to the game tonight? I knew Mom wasn't feeling well, but my neighbor, Linda, said she'd check in on her. If I didn't want to see Derek so badly, I would've stayed home, but I couldn't wait any longer. Thank God, Linda helped me out. Finding Mom panicking must've scared the pants off her.

I punch the seat beside me and give the car we passed the finger.

However, I wish she hadn't waited until the third period to call me.

"Get out of the way, loser!" I yell at the car in front of us. This won't help my Uber rating, but I don't care. I just need to get to Mom.

The entire ten-minute drive, my thoughts are stuck on the what-ifs. What if I had been there, maybe I could've helped her and she wouldn't need to be in the hospital. What if she doesn't recover from whatever this is? These thoughts aren't productive.

I complete the payment for the driver before pulling up at the entrance to the ER. Running out of the car, I make my way to the admissions desk and cut in front of three people waiting to be seen.

"Excuse me," I say to the receptionist, breathless.

The woman with short, spiky brown hair, huge purple plastic glasses, and multiple facial piercings looks up at me and says, "Hold on a sec, hon. I'll be right back." She stands up to walk away.

"No! Please wait."

She turns around, her brows pinched together seemingly into a dark caterpillar-like unibrow. "You're going to have to give me a minute. Nature calls."

Slamming my fist down on the desk, I say, "My mother was brought here in an ambulance. Could you please tell me where she is before I come back there and look on your computer myself?" I'm seconds from crying and she must hear it in my voice or see it in my eyes.

The receptionist pushes her glasses higher up on her nose and walks back to the computer. "What's your mother's name, hon?"

I tell her and she points me in the direction of the intensive care unit.

Cold sweat breaks out over my body before I knock on the door to her room. A tall, thin, gray-haired man comes to the door. He's wearing a white coat and a name badge. "Hello, are you Adeline's family?"

"Yes...I'm...her daughter," I say.

My mom is lying on the bed, sleeping. She's paler than normal and the dark circles under her eyes seem a deeper shade of blue. She's wearing an oxygen mask, and her chest rises and falls in sync with the beeping of a machine. There's an IV in her arm delivering clear fluid into her body.

He reaches for my hand and we shake. "My name is Dr. Brown and I've been taking care of your mother. Your neighbor filled me in on what happened. She just left before you got here."

The strong smell of antiseptic hits me and my head starts to feel light and my knees weaken. "Can I sit down?" I don't wait for his answer and sit in the blue chair next to Mom's bed. "Is she going to be okay?"

"How are you feeling? Your face just went white." Dr. Brown gets closer to me, squatting down to look into my eyes.

"No, I'll be fine. What about her?" My tone is clipped.

He stands back up to his full height. "She's stable, but she did have a stroke. She's unable to talk and it's affected her right side."

"She's going to get it back though, right?"

He shakes his head and reaches for her chart at the end of her bed. Leafing through the papers, he stops and reads through a page. "Unfortunately, it's unlikely that she will, especially with her MS."

There's a sharp sting behind my eyes before the tears start falling. "What do we do now?"

Dr. Brown's eyes are kind and sympathetic. He gets a tissue out of the box on the side table and hands it to me. "Your mother was confused when she came in. We gave her some medicine to help her rest. It'll be good for her brain if she doesn't get upset tonight. Why don't you go home and get some rest? Come back first thing tomorrow. I'll be going over her case first thing with my colleagues and have more information for you."

I nod because I'm in shock and don't know what else to say or do. Her room doesn't look like there's anywhere for me to lie down comfortably. Of course I don't want to go, but it looks like I don't have much of a choice.

Grasping my mom's cold hand in mine, I swallow the lump

forming in my throat and tell her, "I'll be back soon, Mom. Don't worry, we'll get this all straightened out." I lay a kiss on her cheek. She doesn't move.

I leave her room and order another Uber to get home. Heading outside, I scroll through my missed calls and texts from Derek. Having silenced my phone before entering the hospital, I didn't realize he was trying to get in touch with me. He has to be worried. I send him a quick message.

Sorry I left the game so quickly. My mom was taken by ambulance to the ER. She's ok. I'm going home to sleep. Talk soon.

Almost immediately Derek calls.

"What can I do?" he asks before I even have the chance to say hello. His voice is so comforting; I almost break down and cry again.

"Hi, there's nothing you can do. But thank you." I do my best to keep my tone light.

"What happened?"

The breeze out here is cool. I zip my jacket up under my chin. "Mom had a stroke, but she's resting comfortably. As much as I'd like to stay, the doctor said I should leave. I'm on my way home now."

"Oh, I'm sorry to hear that. Can I come and give you a ride?"

"I already ordered an Uber. It will be here any second. You must be exhausted from your game. Go home. We can talk tomorrow," I tell him, pacing back and forth in front of the hospital.

"I'm leaving tomorrow afternoon. I'll meet you at the hospital in the morning. How does that sound?" There's a ding in the background. Sounds like the microwave. He's probably heating up his favorite, post-game chimichangas.

"That'd be great." I smile to myself. Of course, he knew I'd be there and I love that he didn't even hesitate to come and be with me before he leaves for his next game.

He sighs into the receiver, "I miss you."

My insides warm up. I'm smitten. "I miss you, too."

We hang up and the Uber pulls up in front of me.

***

"I THINK it's the way you like it." Derek hands me a large coffee outside my mother's hospital room. His other hand holds a huge bouquet of flowers—pink roses, daisies, and sunflowers.

A dumb grin forms on my face. "You have no idea how much I need this. I barely slept a wink." I tossed and turned all night thinking about my poor mother lying in a hospital bed without me. It's impossible not to feel guilty about not being with her last night. She must've been terrified.

Derek pulls me into his warm arms. I sink into him and let the comfort wash over me. "It's all going to be okay." His hand massages my back, wiping the tension away with each stroke.

I want to believe him.

With some hesitation, I pull away, not wanting to let go of this security. "We should go in. I don't want Mom to be alone for too long. I got here at six a.m. and she was awake. She had a small smile on half of her face when she saw me. I've been by her side ever since. Until I got your call." I give him a shrug. "She doesn't look great with the oxygen and tubes, but she seems to be in good spirits."

He places his hand on my back. "Let's go in."

I open the door and we head in. I take my seat next to my mom and grab her hand again. "Look who came to visit."

Derek stands on the other side of me and Mom gives him the same half smile she gave me.

"I wanted to come see you before I leave this afternoon." He rubs Mom's left hand.

"Isn't that sweet, Mom?"

The door swings open and a middle-aged woman with long

dark hair and a white coat comes in. She shakes both Derek's and my hand. "Hi, I'm Dr. Davis."

We introduce ourselves and she checks the monitors and computer. "I'm going to go talk to your daughter, Adeline. We'll be right back." She picks up the chart at the end of the bed.

Mom nods and Derek and I go to the hallway with Dr. Davis.

Derek holds my hand and we lean against the wall. The comfort of Derek's strong grip soothes my nerves.

"I'm glad you're here. I've spoken with Dr. Brown and we've gone over your mother's case." She pushes her black-framed glasses up further on her nose. "Her prognosis isn't good when you take into account her history. We did a CT scan and found that there was an obstruction within one of the blood vessels. It damaged the area in her brain that controls motor function. She's going to have difficulty using the right half of her body, including swallowing, speech, and movement of her arms and legs. I expect her to regain some function, but unfortunately she won't recover fully."

"Okay," I say, numbly.

She reaches into the chart and pulls out a few brochures. "These are the assisted living homes in the area. Your mother will need 'round the clock care. She likely will need a feeding tube and assistance with her basic daily needs."

I take the brochures and my stomach drops to the ground and tears start falling fast and hard.

"Some of the homes are subsidized and others are quite expensive. Take the brochures home and decide what makes most sense for you and your budget. I'm here to assist you in any way you need. I'll be back in a couple of hours after rounds to see Adeline again." She gives me a sympathetic smile and walks down the hall.

My legs want to give out and my chest heaves from crying.

Derek is right there bringing me into his embrace. "I'm going to help you."

Nothing but the best, that's what my mother deserves. There is no other way. "Please help us," I mutter into his chest.

His strong arms and masculine scent wrap me in a blanket of comfort and safety. "It's done. I'm so sorry that I have to leave today, but I'll get things in the works for your mom at Riverview." His breath tickles the top of my head.

I clutch the fabric of his sweater as though it can ground me here. Deep inside, I know I can't take care of my mother on my own anymore and it stings like a thousand open wounds. And Derek is the healing balm, ready to help alleviate the pain in any way he knows how. I wish he didn't have to leave so soon.

Right now in the hallway of the cold, sterile hospital, I could tell Derek that I love him and mean it fully and completely. It's foolish and too soon, but I can't deny what I'm feeling. I don't open my mouth to speak, instead I press my lips to his and kiss him deeply, like we're the only two people on Earth, and for the moment, I'm swept away in Derek and the sanctuary he provides.

***

HOURS AFTER DEREK LEAVES, Bri stops by Mom's hospital room with a bouquet of pink and white lilies.

"Thank you for coming." I take the flowers from her and set them next to Derek's on the windowsill. "Maybe Mom will wake up while you're here. She's been resting for a little over an hour now."

"Let her sleep. Her body needs it. How's she doing?" Bri takes the seat at the end of Mom's bed and crosses her legs.

Frowning, I sigh and plop into my spot to the right of Mom. "I wish I could say things were going better, but the stroke did some damage. I'm not sure if she'll walk or talk again." Tears form at the corners of my eyes.

Lifting her chair, she brings it next to mine and grabs my hand. "It's going to be okay."

I love her comforting words even if she has no idea if things will be okay or not. Grabbing another tissue, I dab my eyes. "Derek is going to help me get her into a room at Riverview. I know she'll be comfortable there. It has top-rated doctors and staff as well as a stroke rehab unit."

Bri is quiet and her gaze points down.

"What's wrong?" I ask.

She scratches her cheek and blows out a long breath. "Damn it. I didn't want to have to be the one to tell you this."

"Now you have to tell me." My voice rises, but not loud enough to alert my mother.

Her gaze ping-pongs around the room and finally lands on mine. "It's Derek's ex. She posted pictures of herself and Derek together last night, arms around each other and another one with the two of them kissing. Looks like they were at a nightclub. The caption read 'Gotta celebrate the big win tonight.'" She tugs her phone out of her purse and pulls up the pictures.

Barely looking, I wince and stand, feeling like I could crawl out of my skin. Pointing toward the door, I say, "Come with me. I need some air."

She follows me down the hall to the elevators and grabs me by the shoulders. "I'm sorry I showed you the pictures. I hate that this is all happening to you now. But I'm here for you. Okay?"

I jab my finger against the down arrow and pace back and forth. "How could he do this?"

"It doesn't make sense. He didn't seem like a player to me," Bri says and walks into the empty elevator.

I shake my head trying to pretend that this is all a bad dream. How could I be so stupid? "He came here today and reassured me that everything would be okay. Told me he'd help get Mom into Riverview. Why would he do that if he's still with Carrie?" The elevator dings at the bottom floor and I almost run to the doors to get outside. As soon as fresh air hits my lungs, I bend at the waist and sob, breathing through the nausea.

Bri rubs my back, her small warm hands moving up and down my spine, and she waits for my fit to end.

Standing up, I wipe my face off with my sleeve. "We never gave ourselves a label so why does this hurt so bad?"

Bri and I head toward an empty bench down on the sidewalk. "You were falling for him, weren't you?"

I take a seat. "How could I not? He and I had a connection that came hard and fast. I've never experienced anything like it. It must've been all fake. I'm such a fool."

"No. Don't do that. You can't blame yourself for this. You're a smart girl. You'd be able to tell if he was pulling the wool over your eyes," she says.

My fingers pick at the material of my jeans. "I might be book smart, but I'm obviously terrible at reading people. Maybe it's time for me to join a convent. No more men for me."

Bri tips her head back and lets out a belly laugh. "From stripper to nun. I can see it now."

I give her arm a playful whack.

"Damn hockey players," she says, shaking her head.

I nod and curse myself for believing he was different.

SLEEPING in the chair next to my mother's bed is for the birds. My lower back is stiff and I can barely move my neck to the right, but it's worth it to me to be here for Mom if she gets up in the night and needs me.

It's no surprise that my boss is an asshole when I call him to tell him what's going on with my mother. Like I wanted this to happen simply so I could inconvenience him. I have to beg him for a few days off and promise him I'll get all of my shifts covered. I'm going to need the time to figure out how to proceed with my mother's care. From the pictures I saw of Derek and Carrie, it looks like I can't rely on him anymore.

I'd like to work up the courage to call him and ask him about Carrie, but I don't have the mental energy at the moment to try and figure out what to say.

Mom is still asleep and I need a caffeine fix. Ambling out of the chair, I get up and make my way to the cafeteria on the first floor. In the elevator, I pull my phone from my pocket and find a text from Derek.

You should be getting paperwork to sign via email today. Email it back and she'll be all set with a private room at Riverview. Miss you. Call me later.

I'm grateful, but at the same time confused and heartbroken. Without a clue of what to say, I simply text back.

Thanks.

He texts back immediately.

How's your mom doing?

She's okay.

That's all I have for him right now.

The line in the cafeteria is short. I take a cup and fill it with the semi-drinkable coffee, adding cream and sugar. Finding a seat by the windows, I sit down and take a sip.

I don't know what to think. When Bri left last night, I promised her I wouldn't look at the photos, but I can't help myself. Pulling up Carrie White's social media account, my stomach sinks.

Derek is standing there in one of the pictures, dark eyes shining, almost glazed over with a huge toothy smile on his face and gorgeous Carrie has her thin arm dangled over his shoulder. In the next shot, their lips are joined together and nausea rolls through me. Such a beautiful couple. It looks like they're at the same nightclub I went to with Bri for an after party.

Carrie posted a picture today, too. It's immediately after a game. He's in his uniform and there's a sheen of sweat covering his face and hair, and she has a jersey on. Definitely a selfie. They're both smiling like they're in a toothpaste ad.

Why am I such a fool?

Staring outside at the dreary sky and leafless trees, my mood seems to match the day. I really thought he was different and wanted to see where things would go with me. But I'm no competition for Carrie White, the supermodel who had his heart first. A tear slides down my cheek. I wipe at it with the back of my hand. The more I think about how far I was falling for him, the more the tears come. This time, I let them. My chest heaves and I ugly-cry for several minutes before I can get up and go to the bathroom to freshen up. I don't want my mother to see me this way.

Waiting for the elevator, I open my email account and find that, as Derek promised, everything is in order from Riverview. It makes no sense. He's actually a good guy, which makes this so much harder. Just when I thought I couldn't cry anymore, more tears begin to fall.

THIRTEEN

Derek

IT'S ALWAYS good to be home, especially after being gone for five days. I can't wait to see Cora. It's been too long since I've held her, touched her skin.

We just landed and my car can't speed home fast enough. Cranking heavy metal music, I tap out the beat on the steering wheel. I need a shower and to see Cora. As soon as possible.

She's been distant, but she's had her hands full taking care of her mother. My uncle really pulled through for me and got Adeline a room at Riverview. There's a wait list a mile long to get in there, but he managed to make it happen. Pays to have connections.

Carrie's been relentless and hasn't let up. She calls and texts me every day now. But the more she tries, the more I realize I made the right choice turning her away. We're so done.

I've tried calling Cora's cell phone twice since we landed.

One last try. I dial her number and let it ring until it goes to voice mail again. Maybe she has to work, or she could be at the hospital still with her mother. I'm not far from her place, so I decide to swing by now.

Her car is in the driveway. I pull in and kill the engine.

Knocking three times, I wait on her porch. There's no answer, but I hear footsteps inside.

I knock again, harder this time. Maybe she has her earbuds in and can't hear me. "Cora," I call out.

Again nothing, but this time the footfalls get closer to the door. "I can hear you in there. It's Derek. Please let me in."

The door opens part way, but the lock is latched. She's standing behind it because I can't see her. "Thank you for all you've done for my mother, but you don't have to pretend you want to be with me anymore. I'm letting you off the hook. Now go away, please."

The tone in her voice stirs up an emotion in me that I haven't felt in a long time. Fear. Something isn't right. "What's wrong, Cora?"

"I'm busy. I can't do this." Her voice sounds depleted and sad.

Holy shit. She's quitting us. "What changed? Why don't you want me anymore?"

Cora lets out a strangled laugh. "No, I can't. Please go away." She's crying now. "I really have to go. Goodbye." And she shuts the door.

I knock, unwilling to accept whatever that just was. She doesn't answer. No footsteps and I can't hear her crying either. It's silent, like she disappeared.

Pain crushes my chest. She's completely shutting me out. Maybe that's why she was distant while I've been away. I'll figure this out, somehow.

Getting back in my car, I sit and watch her house. No movement inside that I can see. I dial Teddy's number and put him on Bluetooth before I drive away.

"Hey, what's up, man? Miss me already?" His crazy laugh bellows through the car.

I don't have time for his humor. "Has Bri mentioned what's wrong with Cora?"

"With Cora? No. Not a word."

"Fuck." I smack the steering wheel with my open palm and pain shoots through my hand to my wrist.

The sound of his television comes through the line, lots of cheering, maybe sports. "What's wrong, man? I thought you and Carrie were getting back together? I've seen her at the games lately and the pictures she's been posting on social media of you two."

"What has she been posting?" I ask, nearly snarling. I'm never on social media. Ever. It's usually a bunch of he said, she said bullshit. It's a waste of my time. Looks like I need to check out what he's talking about when I get home.

"It's pictures of you guys together kissing and stuff."

No. No. No. I slam the brakes as I turn into a gas station and pull up Carrie's social media account. That soulless woman has been posting photos from last year. But it looks like they happened in the last few days and the caption reads, 'me and my guy.' "Damn it. Why is she fucking doing this?" Rage bubbles up in me and I open the door and spring out to pace and diffuse some of the fury.

"She wants you back, man. I thought that was what you wanted." That's what I did want. But since I've reconnected with Cora, things have changed.

"Not anymore. I want Cora. This shit with Carrie has to stop," I spit out.

There's loud cheering in the background and the sound of Teddy clapping his hands together.

"What are you watching, man?" I ask, annoyed that he isn't fully here in the conversation.

The crowd noise gets lower. "Sorry. I DVR'd the football game. Watching the playback now. Anyway, why don't you call Carrie and tell her to fuck off, then call Cora and tell her you want to fuck." He lets out a low chuckle.

"And how is it you're still single?" The dude is completely clueless when it comes to women.

I get back in my car and put Teddy back on Bluetooth.

"Now that you mention it, I was going to ask you for some dating advice. I'd like to date Bri, but I don't know how." His voice takes on a pouty tone.

Letting out a deep breath, I pull out of the gas station and drive toward the highway. "I don't know if I'm the right person to ask at the moment, but why don't you call her and tell her you want to get together, go out on dates? Do nice things for her like send her flowers or leave her notes. Listen to her when she talks; don't be distracted by a football game. It should start to come natural to you."

Teddy says, "Oh, that sounds easy." It's almost as if I can hear the lightbulb go off over his head.

"It can be. And you two seem to be getting along every time you're together. You thinking about being exclusive?" It would be a first. The guy's never had a serious girlfriend since I've known him.

"I think so. She's a cool chick. And I'm interested in getting to know her and not just get in her pants. Weird, huh?" He sounds sincere.

Pulling into the driveway, I turn the engine off. "Good for you, man. I have to run and deal with my shit. See you at practice in the morning."

"Thanks," Teddy says before hanging up.

I squeeze the muscles of my neck and take a few calming breaths before I get out of my car. This is the last place I want to be, but it has to be done once and for all.

Knocking on her door, I wait, tapping my foot.

A smile spreads across her face like I'm holding a check and she won the Publisher's Clearinghouse Sweepstakes. "You're here. Come in."

"It's best if you come out here." I don't want to get trapped in her house. Who knows what stunts she'll try and pull now that I'm here?

The smile that was there seconds ago has disappeared into a scowl. She's dressed in a pair of short shorts and a skimpy tank top. No bra. I know I'm over her because the sight of her perky nipples used to make me want to suck on them until they were red and sore. Not at all today. "Please, come in. My neighbors already know enough of my business." She turns and walks inside.

Even though I know it's a bad idea, I follow her because I know her stubborn ass won't talk to me out here. I don't get one step past the threshold with the door shut and I stop. "I'm staying here."

She was going toward her living room, but she stops and looks over her shoulder. Realization dawns on her face. She wanted me in here, well, here I am, but I won't go any further. She comes back to stand in the foyer with me. "Why won't you come in?"

Pushing my hands into my jeans pocket, I say, "This will be quick. We're done, Carrie. You filed the paperwork. We both signed it. I don't want to get back together."

Her jaw hangs open, like this is news to her. "What do I have to do to change your mind?"

She gets closer to me and I put my hands up. "Don't touch me. This has all got to stop. There's nothing you can do." My tone is even. I'm doing my best not to lose my shit. You get nowhere with her once the yelling starts.

"Why are you being so unreasonable?" she huffs.

Squeezing my palms together, I say, "Why are you posting old pictures on the Internet and acting like we're still together?"

She turns her head away from me and blinks rapidly. "I love all of those pictures. What's wrong with me posting them?"

I hate when she plays coy like this. It's fucking annoying and makes me want to throw shit. Not productive. "Remember when you told me that it was time to let go? Back when you served me the divorce papers? Well, now it's time for you to take your own advice. Let me go."

Tears stream down her thin cheeks and she leans her hip against the console table. "Fuck. This hurts."

"It does, but you'll move on and find happiness again," I say with confidence in my tone. It's the only comfort I can offer her.

"Do you love her? The woman from the pictures?" she asks between sobs.

"Carrie. This isn't going to help anything." My patience is waning.

She wipes under her eyes with the bottom of her shirt, exposing her tight abs. I turn my head. "You're right. You deserve to be happy, Derek."

"So do you. And do you know what would make me really happy?"

She looks at me through damp lashes. "What?"

"If you could take down the old pictures. Or at the very least, don't post anymore. I'm moving on and you know holding onto the past isn't going to help you move forward either."

She walks the two steps toward me and throws her arms around me. Her touch and scent do nothing anymore. No spark ignites. It's a good feeling. I hug her back, but only for a moment.

"I have to go. Take care of yourself." Turning, I clutch the door handle in my hand.

"Goodbye," she says.

Getting in my car, a peace comes over me.

I know now what I have to do.

FOURTEEN

Cora

A HORN HONKS. Peeking out my window, it's Bri's car in my driveway.

Grabbing my clutch from the counter, I head out the front door as fast as my heels and black party dress will allow.

I get in the passenger seat and say, "Thanks for driving."

"No problem. That dress is gorgeous," she says, eying me with a mischievous grin.

Bri's hair is pulled up in a high ponytail and her makeup is flawless. "You look great, too."

"I love bachelorette parties," she says as she puts the car in reverse and backs out of my driveway.

My stomach sinks. Normally, I like a good bachelorette party as much as the next girl. Getting a little crazy with girlfriends, having some drinks, and flirting with men is always a good time. But when Rose called me up to invite Bri and me to her bachelorette party, I thought I shouldn't accept. I haven't talked to Derek in a week. Not since that day at my house. It doesn't seem right to be hanging out with his friend's fiancée. "Are you sure this is a good idea?"

She waves her hand at me. "Of course it is. Remember that Rose invited us to come."

"She doesn't know that Derek and I aren't together anymore. And what if Carrie shows up?" The thought of seeing her makes me nauseous.

Bri sighs. "She won't be there. I still think that bitch isn't getting back together with Derek. She hasn't posted on social media in a week. You need to hear him out."

My heart wants me to go talk to Derek, but my head is telling me it's a bad idea and I'll end up hurting worse than I am now. "I will. He reached out at the beginning of the week and left a voice message asking me to meet him for coffee."

I've listened to the message over and over again. His voice sounds sad; it breaks my heart to hear him like that. But what if I go to see him and he tells me that he and Carrie hooked up, or worse that they're getting back together? I don't have any claim over him, but I was falling for him nonetheless.

I've been an absolute wreck. Every day I want to pick up the phone and call him. It's been torture not seeing him as well. Maybe it'll get easier as time goes on. That's what I'm hoping for.

Bri pulls onto the highway and hits the accelerator. I nearly get whiplash from the speed change. She's always been a crazy driver. "Good. Do it for yourself and for Derek. He deserves to have a conversation with you. Teddy did mention that Derek hasn't been himself lately."

My head spins from everything that's been going on in my life lately. My mom's stroke, the photos of Carrie and Derek, and most recently, Steve putting me on probation at Lolita's. He said I didn't get all of my shifts covered and didn't call in for one of them. Things were chaotic. I thought I took care of everything. At least he didn't fire me. "I can relate. What about you and Teddy? You guys are still in regular contact."

She signals, cuts over past two cars, and pulls off our exit. "He's been putting in effort, but I'm not looking to get serious. It's too soon after my divorce."

I can smell it. She's afraid. Can't blame her. "Maybe you should take your own advice. Live day by day. Stay out of your head."

Whipping her head in my direction, she gives me an irritated grin. She's never liked being called out. "Oh, look, we're here." She buzzes into the parking lot at lightning speed and slams the car into park. "Let's go. I need a drink."

Guess the conversation is over. We get out of the car and make our way to the entrance of Posh, an exclusive nightclub in the city. I've never been here and the nerves kick in when we walk in the place.

It's massive. Two floors, on the first there are two long bars along the back and left walls. The rest is a massive dance floor with people bumping and grinding to the steady beat of the dance music. Bri takes my hand and guides me upstairs. The music isn't quite as loud up here. Three of the walls are floor-to-ceiling windows with a bar in the center.

Rose and the other ladies are gathered around a big table. She sees us and comes running over. "You made it." She throws her arms around me.

"I love your dress," I tell her. She's in a maroon V-neck lace dress with spaghetti straps donning a "Bride" sash.

Twirling around, she nearly spills the contents of her champagne flute. "Thank you. Now come, get a drink."

Bri and I follow her to the table where there are bottles of champs and wine. We each get a glass of red and Rose makes introductions. We already met Lydia, Wes's girlfriend and country singer extraordinaire, but you'd never know she was a celebrity from her attitude—but the huge bodyguard standing nearby her might give it away. She's sweet and down to earth. We meet Rose's sister and various other friends of hers, who all seem friendly and welcoming to Bri and me, the newcomers.

I mingle with the ladies and my first glass of wine goes down quickly. I pour myself a second glass and drink half of it. Nothing like some wine to take the edge off.

Rose grabs me by the arm and says, "We're going downstairs to dance. Come with us."

Emptying my glass, I tell her, "Sure. Let's go."

On the dance floor, we find an opening that will allow us all to be together. Rose has some moves; the woman knows how to shake her booty. I tone down the dancing I do for my stripagrams to keep it respectable.

Bri shakes her booty against mine and we shimmy together to the beat. I haven't been out dancing with girlfriends in a long time and it feels so good to let loose and forget about my problems for a couple of hours.

Sweat mists my forehead and I know it's time for another drink. I lift my arm to the group, giving them the I-need-a-drink signal and make my way back upstairs for another. Rose follows close behind me.

"I've been wanting to chat with you alone all night." Rose gives me a warm smile that reaches all the way up to her eyes and it lands smack dab in my heart. She has such great energy.

"Yeah. Tell me, what's up?" I grab a glass and pour myself some wine.

She lifts the champagne bottle and fills herself up and raises it in the air. "Cheers and thanks for being here."

"Of course. No place I'd rather be. Your friends are so much fun," I say.

Rose runs her thin hand through her hair and cocks her head to the side. "Please don't think I'm trying to butt into your relationship. I know that we haven't known each other long, but Rick and Derek have been friends for years. Tell me if I am over-stepping."

The hairs on the back of my neck stand up. "Ok, you're making me nervous."

She lays her hand on my arm. "No, it's nothing like that. I want to tell you what a good guy Derek is. Rick told me that Derek has been a wreck lately because you guys aren't talking."

I nod. "He's back with Carrie. Did Rick tell you that?" Tears sting the back of my eyes.

Her eyes widen and she takes me by the shoulders. "No, he isn't. Are you talking about the old pictures that she was posting recently?"

Wait. Old photos? "I thought they were new. She just posted them last week."

"Carrie is evil. She's trying to get him back, but he doesn't want her. He wants you."

A knot forms at the back of my throat. Could this be true? It makes sense. Maybe this is what he wanted to tell me, but I've been too caught up in my own shit to give him a chance to explain. "Are you kidding me?"

"No, I'm serious." She lifts her head and meets my gaze. "You should give him another shot. He cares about you."

I try to suppress my smile, but it doesn't work. My entire body smiles. "I would love that."

Rose's sister comes up to the table with the rest of the group, holding a tray full of shot glasses. She hands each of us one and yells, "To the bride!"

We tilt our glasses back and slam the clear liquid. Tastes like vodka. It burns down the back of my throat. I'm loose and relaxed and extremely excited that Derek and Carrie aren't getting back together.

Back out on the dance floor, I have my arms in the air feeling the music when a hard body presses up flush against mine. I spin around to find him standing in front of me with a black button-up shirt on, jeans, and the sexiest grin on his face.

FIFTEEN

Cora

"HI," Derek says.

"Hi." My breath hitches.

"Want to dance with me?" he asks, but his hands are already around my waist and he's pulling me in close.

My arms go around his shoulders. "I didn't know you were coming."

His mouth is next to my ear and he lays a gentle kiss there, making my knees go weak. "Are you okay with me being here?"

I tilt my head to the side, exposing my neck for him, hoping he'll take the bait. "It's a free country."

He laughs and his warm breath skims my shoulder. His tongue makes a languid stroke from the back of my ear toward my collar bone.

A pulse forms between my legs and I grip the back of his hair in my hands. I've missed this. He knows exactly what to do to me to get me going.

We sway together to the music and it's just him and me. Nobody else in the world matters. He looks at me with his intense dark eyes and I'm completely entranced. His hands come up to cup my cheeks and his lips move over mine, softly at first until his tongue plunges in my mouth. My core clenches with need.

"Maybe we should leave," I say, my voice coming out breathy and my chest heaving.

He pulls back, a devilish smile on his face. "Looks like you ladies are having a good time. Have you had a few drinks?"

My hands clutch the fabric of his shirt. "Oh, yeah. I'm drunk, but I still want you to take me home."

"I'd like that." He lays a soft kiss on my cheek. "Why don't you say goodbye to everyone and I'll drive you home."

Unwilling to leave the sexual haze Derek has me in, I say, "It'll be quick."

That cute laugh of his again. He grasps my hand in his and leads me toward Bri. I give her a thumbs up and wind my arm around Derek's. She gives me a wicked grin and a thumbs up back.

The short ride home, I'm practically crawling all over him. There's no talking. I'm kissing his face, his neck. At one point during a stoplight, I'm in his lap, grinding on him, my tongue down his throat. A honk from behind us triggers me to get off him.

Standing up to get out of the car once we're at my house, the world seems to be tipped off its axis and I stumble to get my footing. Derek is right there next to me. "You okay?" he asks.

"I'll be good." Clutching onto his arm, I use him for support while we make our way to the house. I pull out my keys and hand them to him. "Could you do the honors?"

He unlocks the door and I lead him to my room. Tugging off

my heels, I throw them in the corner and lie down, patting the spot next to me. "Come here," I say.

The room spins. I close my eyes and wait for the world to stop moving.

Derek lays next to me. "Are you sure you're all right?" he asks, running his fingers through my hair.

I nod and slowly open my eyes. "Thanks for bringing me home. I'm glad you came."

"I'm glad you're glad I came." He lays a gentle kiss on my lips. "You've been avoiding me. Do you want to talk about it, or is this a bad night for that?"

Placing my arm under my head, I get myself comfortable. "No. It's the perfect night. I'm sorry that I didn't give you a chance to explain yourself. I was too busy and caught up in my own crap and didn't give you a chance. I should've."

He licks his lips and nods. "I wasn't going to let you give up on us that easy. After I saw the pictures that Carrie was posting—from last year—I might add, I knew what you must've been thinking. And of course, I know you've been under a great deal of pressure after your mother's stroke. You shouldn't have shut me out."

Guilt floods me. Of course he's right, but I was being too stubborn to get out of my own way. "Can you forgive me?"

"It's already done." His fingertips graze my lips. "But you can't pull that shit anymore. Talk to me."

I nod, unable to look away from his gorgeous dark eyes. "I promise."

"Good. Because I can't worry that when things get rough you're going to shut me out. Or worse, run." A flash of dread passes over his features.

My heart hurts. That's what Carrie did. I don't want him to have an ounce of fear that I'll turn my back on us. "Derek." I pull his shirt up and place my palms flat on the smooth skin of his chest. "I was starting to fall for you. And when I wasn't talking to you, I missed you so much."

A grin tugs at the corner of his mouth and his thumb caresses my cheek. "I feel the same. Tell me you're ready to be exclusive with me. I don't want anyone else."

Tears slip down my cheek to my pillow. "I don't want anyone else either, but are you sure you want to be with someone like me? I don't have my life together."

His finger swipes away the dampness on my cheek. "It wrecks me when you cry. There's no need for tears. I don't care if you don't have your life all figured out. I can help you."

"From day one you've been trying to help me. But what am I doing for you?" I ask.

He cups my jaw in his hand. "You give me so much. Can't you see that? You challenge me, you get me. I don't know anyone smarter than you are. And don't get me started on how insanely attracted to you I am. I get hard in my dreams when I think about you."

A laugh bubbles up. "I want to be your perfect partner. Someone who has pride in her job."

He clasps my palm and interlaces his fingers in mine and brings our hands to his mouth, kissing the back of mine. "Why don't you go back to college? Get your law degree. Now that your mom is safe and settled with the care she needs, you can start thinking about yourself."

I worry at my bottom lip, running my teeth over it. How could I afford to do that? It'd be difficult. The house is paid for, but not utilities. I'd have to pay for my car insurance and food, too. "I don't know if I could make it work."

"You already know how to make it work. You're one of the strongest, smartest people I've ever met. And I know you don't want to take anymore of my help, but I'm here for you. I have more money than I know what to do with. I'd love to help my math tutor follow her dreams."

The tears fall faster now. "Maybe I could do it. I'm afraid I'm going to lose my job at Lolita's anyway. My boss, Steve, hasn't taken my calls in the last two days. But I could apply for financial aid."

"Screw Lolita's. You could always find something part-time at a nice Italian restaurant or something. Anything but the stripa-grams. I'm pretty secure in my manhood, but knowing you're going out to bachelor parties and taking off your clothes for dirty-minded men who want to bend you over and fuck you would be more than I think I can handle." He's smiling, but I can see in the set of his jaw that he's serious.

"Thank you," I tell him. "For being patient with me and encouraging me. I want to be a lawyer. I'm going to look into it and see if I can manage it."

His eyes take me in with wonder, like I'm the most beautiful, intelligent woman he's ever seen. "That's my girl." He tugs me in closer and I melt into him.

Pulling back, I angle my face toward his and place a kiss on his lips. He cups the nape of my neck and deepens the kiss. Closing my eyes, I wait to see if the room spins. It doesn't. Maybe the conversation sobered me up. "I want you," I whisper, barely breaking the kiss.

He tugs my dress up and I lean on one elbow to help get it over my head. He takes off my bra and underwear and tosses them on the floor. I shamelessly watch as he pulls off his shirt, pants, and boxers.

Lying back down, he hovers over me. His tongue traces my lips and dips in my mouth. He nips and teases me, creating a deep need in my core. "All I could think about was this when we weren't together. But I never jerked off."

My eyes widen at his confession. "Why not?"

"It wouldn't be worth it. I craved your skin, your mouth, your touch. This is what I needed." His hand comes up and cups my breast, squeezing my nipple between his fingers.

I moan and arch into his touch. He drags his finger slowly down my stomach all the way down to my sex. My skin tingles everywhere he touches me. Plunging two fingers in, his thumb works my clit. Derek sucks on my neck and my belly clenches. "I love how wet you are for me." He nearly growls.

"That feels so good, but I want you inside me. Please," I practically beg.

He's up and off my bed, digging in his pocket. He pulls out a condom, rips it open, and sheaths himself. He's back on the bed, balancing over me. His thick length aligned with my opening. "Did you miss this, too?" His voice is hoarse like he's hovering on the edge.

"So much." I grasp the curve of his ass and apply downward pressure as I raise my hips up.

Sinking into me, he tilts his head back and groans. "You're perfect. Nothing feels as good as you."

The heat of his body against mine and his smell intoxicate me. I drag my fingers up his back and into his hair; the strands are soft and silky to the touch.

He flips us over and I'm straddling him. "I want you to ride me," he says, breathless.

My hands clutch his chest and I rock up and down his length. He reaches under and grips my ass and guides me, controlling the rhythm. He pounds up into me, hitting the sweet bundle of nerves deep inside. One of his hands comes up and works my clit with skilled pressure.

My orgasm blindsides me. A rush of pleasure surges through me. I cry out his name as spasm after spasm cascade over me.

I take him in, every beautiful inch. I don't know how I got so lucky, but I won't take it for granted. His eyes are lidded and his mouth is parted. His abs get rigid and stiff seconds before he shudders.

"Cora," he breathes out and pulses into me.

I lie on him, my breasts against his hard chest and kiss him. It's several minutes before we come down from the high.

Derek's fingertips make sweeping circles on my back and my eyelids get heavy. Laying my cheek on his chest, I say, "Stay with me tonight."

"I'm not going anywhere."

SIXTEEN

Derek

"This is the last of it," I tell Cora as I set the box on the floor of Adeline's new room at Riverview.

The room is large by assisted living standards. She has a bed in one corner with a white comforter and all the walls are painted white. There are blinds for the two windows in the room and, you guessed it, white curtains. It has a clean and disinfected feel. That's why Cora wanted to bring some of her mother's favorite items to liven the place up a bit.

"Great. Thanks." She's organizing the windowsill with a few framed pictures of their family.

I've helped her pack up a few of her mother's belongings and bring them over to her room. It's been emotional for Cora, but I've been here for her through all of it over the last couple of weeks.

"Look at this one, Mom." She carries a picture of her and her parents in Rome, the Coliseum behind them. "Wasn't this the best trip? It was in August. We were so hot. I think we ate gelato five times a day to stay cool."

Her mom smiles: half of her face tugs up, the other side is immovable, and she nods. She's been improving and has regained some of her function, but still is fed through a feeding tube.

It's been a hard pill for Cora to swallow, that her mom needs to be here, but she knows that her needs are far beyond Cora's scope now.

We empty her mother's favorite books onto the bookshelf in the corner and scatter a few trinkets and knick-knacks around. She has figurines of herons and owls all over. Cora also brought a brightly colored quilt for her bed.

"Looks homey in here," I say.

Cora's hands are on her hips as she scans the room, and then a smile forms on her face. "It does, doesn't it, Mom?"

Adeline nods her head.

Cora sits on the edge of the bed and squeezes her mother's leg. "Don't worry. I'm going to be here all the time. Remember we have a wedding to go to tomorrow, so I'll stop by in the morning before we go. Ok?"

Her mom nods and smirks.

I gather up the boxes to take with us on our way out. "See you in the morning, Adeline."

"Bye, Momma," Cora says and follows me out the door.

Down the hallway, she puts her arm around me. "Thanks for being here for all of this. You've helped make this transition easier for me."

"I'm here for you. But... I know a way you could repay me when we get back to your place." I wiggle my eyebrows at her, lightening the mood. It's been heavy long enough.

Licking her lips, she says. "That can be arranged."

NORMALLY SITTING through full Catholic mass wedding

ceremonies feels long and tedious. Not today. I listened to the priest talk about love and the sanctity of marriage and it struck a chord with me. I thought what I had with Carrie was what love was supposed to feel like. Now I know how different real love is. With Carrie it was passion and lust and a whirlwind of constant chaos. That's not what it feels like with Cora. This is different. Of course, we have passion—fuck, I can't keep my hands off her— but we're settled and content in the day to day instead of always looking for more. There's a safety in it that I don't take for granted.

Slick and Rose's wedding is beautiful from the flowers at the church to the decorations at the reception, but nothing is quite as gorgeous as my date. Sometimes it's hard to catch my breath with her next to me. We're sitting at the reception now, enjoying dinner. She's in a pale pink number and half of her hair is swept up off her shoulders, exposing one of my favorite spots on her body to kiss, under her ear. My dick twitches in my dress pants when she turns toward me and licks her lips. She knows I'm staring at her. I can't help it.

We continue to grow closer every day, even when I'm out of town for games. We make the effort whether it's a call, a text, a note left behind, or an evening spent Skyping while we eat dinner. It's important to each of us to make this work.

Cora eats the last bite of her salmon and sets her fork down.

"Dance with me," I say. I'm not a big dancer, but I know Cora loves it and it's an excuse for me to touch her.

Her blue eyes light up and she takes the napkin off her lap and sets it aside. "I'd love to."

Reaching out my hand to her, she grasps it and we walk to the dance floor hand in hand. I wrap my arms around her slim waist and stare into her eyes. She gives me an adoring smile that I feel deep in my chest.

We sway in time with the music and over Cora's shoulder,

Slick and Rose are dancing close. He catches my eye and gives me a thumbs up. I wink at him and smile. I couldn't be happier for the guy. He and Rose complement each other so well. She's the calm to his storm. Today's been the perfect day for them.

Not too far off are Teddy and Bri. The two of them look close, even though neither one of them can figure out how to handle the other. Maybe they'll get it. Teddy told me he'd like to date her exclusively.

Cora kisses my jaw and says, "I love weddings."

"Oh, yeah? Do they make you as horny as they do me?" I laugh, but I'm only half joking.

She playfully swats my chest, but she gives me that smile. It disarms me. I take her hand in mine and press it to my chest. "Do you have any idea how incredible and strong you are? And how fucking happy you make me?" I pull her closer to me. Weddings obviously bring out the sap in me.

"Really?" Her fingers graze my cheek and my heartbeat kicks up a notch.

"Yes. And being here today makes me realize that I can't let another second go by without me telling you that I'm proud of you. For taking care of your mom when she needed you, and now for taking the steps to follow your dreams. You're going to kick ass in law school. I know it." She already got accepted back into the program she left five years ago. My heart beats wildly in my chest before I say, "And I love you."

The air between us seems to sizzle as we stare into each other's eyes. "I don't want you to think I'm saying this just to say it, but I love you, too." Her voice comes out as sweet and smooth as the perfect pass in front of the net. I shouldn't be surprised that she's saying the words out loud. She's already shown me. It's in the way she looks at me, like I'm the only man on earth. In the way she holds me and touches me. In the thoughtful little things she does, like the notes she leaves in my suitcase that I find when

I'm at an away game. This is what I've always wanted. She is what I need.

"I don't think you're saying it just to say it. I know you mean it." I lean down and suck her bottom lip into between mine. "How long do we have to stay here today? I'm desperate to take you home and get you out of this dress."

"Oh, are you now? I think we can get going." She clutches my shirt in her hand and tugs me in closer to kiss me again. It's deep and full of promise.

"Let's go and stay in bed for the next two days." My hands move down her waist and grab the top of her round ass.

She shakes her head. "Didn't I tell you, I have the lunch shift tomorrow at Nonna's Kitchen."

I sigh deeply. "Right. That's okay. We have all night tonight and I plan to show you just how horny you've made me in that dress all day." My beautiful, stubborn girlfriend refuses to let me help her pay her bills. At least she isn't taking off her clothes for money anymore and got a job at a local Italian restaurant instead. The tips are good and she likes her co-workers.

"May I have your attention, please?" A man's voice says over the microphone.

Cora and I turn to find the asshole, Marcus Reid, standing next to the DJ stand with microphone in hand and his girlfriend, Alex, is next to him. She's peering around, her hands by her sides, most definitely looking uncomfortable to be standing there with all of the attention on her.

"I wanted to take a second to congratulate the newlyweds on their wedding. Alex and I wish them all the best." Marcus raises his glass and continues, "Cheers to Rose and Rick. May you have a long and happy marriage." He takes a sip of his drink and many others around the room do, too. He sets his glass down and stands in front of Alex. "And in the spirit of the wedding today, I want to tell my stunning girlfriend just how happy she makes me." He drops down to one knee and pulls a box out of his jacket pocket and opens it. "Will you do me the honor of marrying me?"

Alex's hands come up to her mouth and tears stream down her face. She nods her head and says, "Yes."

Marcus slips the ring on her finger. When she holds it up and twirls it, it sparkles in the dance floor lights, sending a kaleido-scope of colors around where she's standing. He lifts her up in his arms and spins her around.

Alex's face is mixture of shock, joy, and dare I say embarrass-ment. Can't blame her. What kind of jerk proposes at someone else's wedding. I'd be humiliated if I were her, too.

Only Marcus Reid would have an ego that big and be completely clueless at the same time.

The wedding attendants cheer and golf-clap. Not Cora and me. We make our way back to our table and take a seat, completely ignoring the spectacle on the dance floor.

Cora's eyes are wide and her lips are a tight line. "Holy shit. Did the asshole that's been cheating on her all along just propose?"

"It appears that he did. Maybe he got it out of his system." I doubt it even as I say it.

"Oh, no. There's zero chance that he's not cheating. Why do you think he's in such a hurry to get married? He's clearly not ready." Her cheeks are getting red and she's gripping her napkin like she wants to choke someone.

Resting my hand on her arm, I say, "Let's not let the biggest asshole on the team ruin our night. Okay?" Everything today has been as close to perfect as it can get. We professed our love for each other and one of my best friends got married. I'm not taking anything for granted and I'll be damned if Marcus is going to wreck it.

She blinks a few times. "You know what? You're right. Let's get out of here." She stands and comes up behind my chair.

Leaning down, she licks my neck. "You mentioned something about wanting to take off my dress," she whispers.

I'm up and out of my chair so fast it scrapes across the floor. Running my hand from her shoulder down her arm to her hand, I clasp it in mine. I take in her gorgeous body, stunning smile, and underneath it all, her huge heart. She's all mine. "Let's say our goodbyes and head out. I'm going to take off your dress with my teeth, and then I'm going to lick your..."

Cora's lips press the corner of my mouth. "If you don't stop now, we aren't going to make it out of the parking lot."

"I love you, Cora."

"I love you, too. Now let's go."

I do as I'm told and lead her out of the reception so I can show her just how much I love her.

The End

IF YOU'RE curious what happens to Alex, check out the next book in the Rules of the Game Series, Defending Your Heart, releasing March 2019.

I'D BE HONORED if you'd leave a review for my story on Amazon. Thank you.

TO KEEP up to date on all of my books, deals and giveaways, sign up for my newsletter here.

ACKNOWLEDGMENTS

First of all, I need to thank my husband, Sam. Without him, none of this would be possible. Period. He's there for me, supporting me, and cheering me on every step of the way through my writing journey. And to my kiddos, you guys are so awesome. I love you both to the moon and back.

A huge hug and thank you to Nicole Andrews Moore, my friend and mentor. You're always there for me and I love you for it. My rock star editor, Theresa Schultz, you make everything better in my stories. Thank you so much. Megan Squiers Parker, thanks for the beautiful cover. Jack looks amazing. To my proofreader, Julie Deaton at Deaton Author Services, you are so good at your job. I swear, nothing gets by you! And to my critique partner, Lisa. You speed read this book for me with the same accuracy and honesty as you would any other of my books. You're invaluable to me.

To all the awesome bloggers out there who work tirelessly to help get the word out there for my books. Because you don't hear it enough, thank you. You deserve all the props for all the hard work you do for authors.

And last but most definitely not least, to my readers. Wow. You're the reason I continue to write stories. Nothing makes me happier than hearing from you guys. It means the world to me that you choose my books to read. Love and hugs to every single one of you.

ABOUT THE AUTHOR

Emma Tharp is the author of *The Bluff Harbor Series, The McLoughlin Brothers Series and Keeping It Casual*. She was raised in upstate New York. Being an only child, she spent a great deal of time alone, dreaming up characters who would keep her company on long family road trips. Putting her writing on the back burner, she went to college and became a chiropractor. After spending twelve years healing patients, Emma decided—with the help of her amazingly supportive husband—to use the creative side of her brain and let her characters come to the page.

If she's not writing, Emma can be found at the gym, one of her kids sporting events, Starbucks, or a live music event.

A perfect day for Emma would be spent at her lake house with her husband, two ginger-haired children, and Vizsla, reading a book and drinking a large cup of coffee (or wine) with music playing in the background.

Contact Emma Tharp at:

www.emmatharp.com

Facebook

Emma's VIP Book Group on Facebook

Twitter

Instagram

Goodreads

Bookbub

Amazon

Other books by Emma Tharp:

What About Her (Book One of the Bluff Harbor Series)
    What About Us (Book Two of the Bluff Harbor Series)
    The McLoughlin Brothers Series Boxed Set

05660

Made in the USA
Lexington, KY
15 February 2019